STARTUP
from the Ground Up

Practical Insights for Entrepreneurs

How to Go From an Idea to New Business

By Cynthia Kocialski

Contents

Prologue

It is the dream of many people—to be an entrepreneur, to start the next company that creates the hottest tech trends, or to change workplaces and lifestyles with a new product. How do you transform your pie in the sky idea into a reality? How do you start? What mistakes should be avoided? Are there any secrets?

The technology and the product is to the start-up what the heart is to the human body: they're critically important, but many other pieces are needed for the human body to function as a whole. A company has no reason to exist without the product, but a great product alone will not make a successful start-up. This book will show what must be wrapped around the technology to create a success story.

All products and businesses emerge and evolve as the start-up interacts with customers, investors, and the marketplace. The successful start-up navigates the process of discovering the product and the business model. This book will show the entrepreneur the key elements of the process and how to let the start-up unfold.

Foreword

I have been involved in more than twenty-four start-ups over the past 15 years. All of these start-ups have been acquired for almost $20 billion. In addition to founding several companies, I have held positions such as COO for start-ups and have served on the advisory board for established companies such as Cypress Semiconductor. I am involved in numerous start-up organizations and groups. I meet with many entrepreneurs about their start-ups and have seen what works and what doesn't. More importantly, the start-up community is ever changing and what worked a few years ago might not work today. The principles of starting a new business stay the same, but the nuances change. Entrepreneurs need to keep in touch not only with their customers and the markets but with the start-up ecosystem.

I did not plan to become a tech entrepreneur, but just like the products involved in all start-ups, my career evolved. I went to graduate school at the University of Virginia. I received two masters degrees in engineering. After several years of teaching computer science to undergraduates and living an academic life, I wanted a more practical application of my field in industry. Upon graduation, my goal was executive engineering management. There was a visiting professor from IBM at the university and he convinced me that IBM would be an excellent place to start my career. In my years at IBM, I worked in three locations developing products from financial software to multi-processor computer systems to components for computer graphics and digital video.

At IBM, I gained expertise in software and hardware development, technical marketing, strategic planning, developing partnerships, conducting business globally before it was trendy, and managing engineering groups. Still, two distinct moments at IBM made it clear that IBM was not the company for me. The first was when I worked for an executive R&D manager in the midst of accelerating his corporate career through extreme political maneuverings. I knew I was more of a performance and results oriented person and far less of an office politician. A short time later, the second moment occurred when my product line was re-organized under a new division. As the person responsible for strategic product planning and representing my product line with the new division, it was clear that the new division had no interest it. My group was unwanted and placed on hold until its fate could be determined. At that point, the entrepreneurial path became a necessity. It was time to move on.

I convinced eight other IBMers to join me in a new venture. These were the key architect, engineers, and programmers. The key architect and I spent six months contacting companies and flying around the country looking for funding. The team knew digital video, a hot commodity at the beginning of MPEG technology. I contacted the President of Micron Computer and one day received a phone call from him. He told me that although Micron wasn't interested, he had mentioned our proposals to the president of another tech company, and they were interested. I had eliminated this company as a possibility because they were outside the U.S. Here was the chance occurrence that got us the deal with Matrox Electronics. It was my next start-up that made me realize how lucky I had gotten with this one—I had put together the right team with management, marketing and engineering experience in the advent of an emerging technology. I was not so lucky with the next start-up.

Eventually the startup settled me back into the role of an employee, as General Manager for an established corporation—a routine, mundane, 9-5 position. I missed the challenge of creating something from nothing. So once again I headed off and co-founded another venture. This time it was a fabless semiconductor company producing low-cost optical networking components. A strategic partnership with FORE Systems, a recent technology IPO and a darling of Wall Street launched this start-up. This start-up only lasted 18 months. It was an enlightening failure. The demise was caused by Gigabit Ethernet; the SONET optical market stalled as everyone waited to see how Gigabit Ethernet would fare in the marketplace. Customers put their orders on hold and investors lost interest. Unfortunately, we had waited to raise more funding until we reached a critical milestone. By then, Gigabit Ethernet was hyped as the one size fits all technology and our start-up ran out of money. Afterwards I realized what we did right as a matter of chance and luck, and what went wrong due to inexperience and purposeful choices. I vowed not to make the same mistakes again. One of my big lessons was to never fight the trend. Instead, embrace the trend and find the opportunity within it.

Afterwards I spent a brief stint as a consultant as a subject matter expert in optical technologies. As the networking and telecom revolution heated up again, the promise of Gigabit Ethernet becoming the end all technology faded and optical networking was hot again. I founded a bootstrapped software company offering networking software to the same customers as the previous start-up. It was a fun ride, lasting seven years until the telecom bubble burst, and the industry plunged into the so-called telecom depression.

The sad truth is there are thousands of start-ups out there and most entrepreneurs create a company that is just a bigger version of the lemonade stand. Here's an illustration of the simple mistakes made over and over again by start-ups. This company's name is Lemon Squeeze, a corner lemonade stand. The budding entrepreneurs have a wonderful idea: provide passerbys with lemonade on street corners. Why this idea? Because the entrepreneurs saw someone else do it, and thought "I can do that too and I'll have an easier time because we have a 40 year old lemon tree in the backyard with too many lemons". A lemonade stand is built quickly with whatever building materials are readily available. But that's not enough; they need more supplies. Simple! The budding entrepreneurs ask their parents for the funds. Once everything is in place, they add a cardboard business sign with the offering, move onto a street corner, and wait for customers. It's an exciting moment when the first customer arrives. This is proof of demand! The lemonade is given away free to anyone who asks. If it was located on a busy street corner on a hot day, keeping up with requests would be difficult. The workers would become overwhelmed making and serving the drinks. The solution is to find more friends to help, but demand would still outstrip production. They are running out of supplies. Now what? Ask Mom and Dad for more funding! But oh no…they are not willing to pay anymore for an operation that's not self sufficient. So the entrepreneurs decide to sell lemonade sips for a quarter because it seems like a nice amount. The price is set on a whim. This is great! Paying customers are even better proof of demand, so they ask for more funding from their parents. The young entrepreneurs are making money, but it isn't enough to cover the cost of goods sold or operating expenses, not to mention paying back Mom and Dad. And Mom and Dad are still not willing to put any more into the operation. Eventually, the lemonade stand runs out of supplies and shuts down operation. The Lemon Squeeze was the brainchild of my first grade daughter.

This book is about making the entrepreneurial dream a reality. It shows an entrepreneur how to go from a product idea to launching a start-up—and not one that is just a lemon stand. I have also been that dreamer. Each time I begin, I believe I can do it better because I have learned from my mistakes and know more about how to avoid the pitfalls.

Introduction

It's More Than the Technology

Thousands of geniuses live and die undiscovered
— either by themselves or by others.

—Mark Twain

A lot of pieces are needed to just get a start-up off the ground, and it's more than just the technical product that makes a start-up successful. This book will set the expectations for the entrepreneur, detail strategies and techniques for success, and shed light on common misconceptions.

This book is an insider's view of start-ups. My first start-up was in 1994. The most surprising revelations in dealing with investors for the first time was how much emphasis there was on the team — their experience, their accomplishments, the successful products in the marketplace associated with team members, and how much emphasis was on the team's knowledge of the market and customers. I have participated in more than 25 start-ups over the years — many successes and numerous failures. These start-ups have returned billions of dollars to investors. After that many start-ups, patterns emerge, mistakes are repeated, and successful methods are repeatedly reproduced. Yet the world is constantly changing and yesterday's successful approach might not work today.

A fundamental confusion about a start-up is what it is and what it is not. If you say the word "start-up" to most people, they envision Microsoft, Apple Computer, Amazon, or Google. These companies are based upon technology. They are scalable in that they started with a single product and grew into very large companies employing thousands of people, with many related products and hundreds of millions of dollars in revenue. They grew to size quickly, often in around 10 years. From their very beginnings, the founders envisioned an organization that could grow into much more than the handful of people who began the company. So while they met the legal definition of a small business early on, they never viewed themselves as small. A small business makes a very tidy livable wage for the owners and it may employ several people, but it will never scale up. In the start-up community, these are currently referred to as life-style businesses. A physician may start a private practice, may employ a few other physicians and a staff, but this practice is not the mammoth Sutter Health. Often founders think they are creating a start-up, but in fact, they are creating a technology-centric small business.

It's not about the product or the technology or the idea; companies don't fail because the product couldn't technically be produced. It's about the creative process of building something when the path is uncertain and the answers aren't clear. A start-up has a life of its own: it is born, it takes it first steps, and it learns and has growing pains. It experiences growing spurts, followed by plateaus, and then more growth. There are no overnight successes. Nothing goes according to plan. What can go wrong will go wrong. What should go smoothly goes roughly. Start-ups don't often realize their first product concept. It's usually a variation, sometimes quite distant from the original idea. The start-up must manage these hiccups, overcome obstacles, adapt to changes, and mature into a profitable and sustainable company. Companies fail more from inadequate strategies than from poor execution of those strategies. Creating and building a company is a process, not an end result.

No two start-ups are the same. The world and circumstances under which start-ups operate is always changing. No one can outline the exact recipe for success. History can provide guidance, but not a step-by-step procedure. If Google were founded today, would it be the success that it is? If Google followed the same steps, it would not be the same company. It might not even be able to obtain seed funding. Google was not the first search engine company. Do you remember Netscape, Alta Vista, Look Smart, and Yahoo? Back then, tech stocks were the darlings of Wall Street, and money was flooding into the start-up community. Seed stage companies were funded with millions of dollars for product ideas sketched on cocktail napkins.

Yesterday, investors wanted to back big projects requiring hundreds of people and hundreds of millions of dollars needed to produce just the non-shippable engineering version of the product. Product development cycles were four years. Today, the typical seed stage companies are funded with only a few hundred thousand dollars, and the advent of micro-financing provides far less financing. Today, start-ups are much smaller, often having less than a dozen people, total investment is a few million, and product development is less than two years. What works for one company today may not work for another company. Success hinges upon subtle nuances. Start-ups are searching for the pieces to their unique puzzle, and the search never ends.

This book is about the early stage. A product idea is inspiring in its simplicity, but converting the idea into a business is complex and riddled with hurdles. An entrepreneur must understand the details and fine points of the business. Miss an important piece to the puzzle and the start-up will vanish.

Gather all the pieces of the puzzle and the start-up may still vanish — or it may become the next household name.

Are You an Entrepreneur?

Flaming enthusiasm, backed up by common sense and persistence is the quality that most frequently makes for success.

—Dale Carnegie

Maybe you want to reap greater rewards for your hard work, or you're tired of working for someone else, or you want to determine your own destiny. Entrepreneurs are not armchair quarterbacks. They thrive on being active participants in the start-up game. They also like to explore and learn new things, to figure out how to create something without instructions. They are not necessarily brilliant people with exceptional industry knowledge and business acumen. They are people who seek out challenges. At some point in the life of every business, there are crises and roadblocks: management predicaments, financial crisis, customer debacles, product issues, personnel problems, public relations fiascos. The only certainty is that the business will not go according to plan. The ability to improvise—quickly and knowledgably—is mandatory. A start-up is unknown to just about everyone. It can dare to be different, to do things in a new way. These differences can be the great advantages of a start-up but every advantage must be fully exploited to win the start-up game.

As an entrepreneur you are the captain of the ship. If the cook in the galley starts a fire, causing a chain of events that sinks the ship, you will be held accountable. The entrepreneur is responsible for the overall performance of the business, but the founders and management cannot make every decision, so hire well.

A crucial characteristic of the entrepreneur is coachability. Founders know they can't do everything; they must make up for their own shortcomings by seeking others with the answers, and they must be willing to listen to experts.

Investors always want to know what keeps an entrepreneur up at night. In other words: what can go wrong—because it will go wrong—and what are the biggest risks? The term "risk management" is often bantered around. It is essentially the method of identifying risks and developing contingency plans to mitigate the unplanned and unanticipated. An entrepreneur's nightmares, the worst and most difficult problems, are identifiable. If the risk can be identified and a response planned, then they are manageable. If globalization has taught anything, it's that the world is very complicated; it's intertwined, and the business eco-system is extremely complex. No one person knows how it is interrelated and how little ripples here or there have great ramifications elsewhere. The most devastating risks are those that cannot be envisioned in one's wildest dreams.

As many have discovered, when you become an entrepreneur, you become unemployable regardless of whether your ventures succeed or fail. Serial entrepreneurs work themselves out of a job because they create and define their own jobs. Failure and success are a matter of perspective — a $100 million acquisition may be a proud accomplishment from a founder's perspective, yet be a dismal disaster from the investor's viewpoint.

Success seems a quick, smooth journey only from an outsider's vantage point. It seems easy from the historical perspective of facts and dates. The first steps are not about the implementation and execution; they're about developing a strategy and discovering the product and company vision. Studies have shown that most business plans fail due to strategy flaws, not execution errors. The key is a commitment to winning.

First-time entrepreneurs are in a hurry. They yearn to get going, they crave for everyone to fall in love with their concept at first sight, they want to get funded today, they need the product development to have been completed yesterday, and they want customers to buy now. Conversely, serial entrepreneurs and seasoned start-up people have learned that success a journey, not a destination, so stop running.

Product and Business Concept

First Steps to Entrepreneurship

Dreamers who make good on their goals have one thing in common: a clear vision of what they want and more importantly, a belief that they can achieve it.

— Marsha Friedman

You've decided to start a company. The good news is you are not forging new ground. Many people have done it before you and best of all, many of them are willing to help people like you.

The first step is to define a product or service that can generate revenue. This may seem basic, but one of the lessons from the dotcom era is there is unlimited demand for anything free. Many would-be entrepreneurs often believe they need a disruptive, revolutionary, or game-changing technology. Likewise, they often believe that first to market is the most desirable. Not true. Many companies simply improve on the business model of their predecessors. Walmart and Target are not new concepts; before these industry giants there was Kmart, and before Kmart were Sears and Montgomery Ward. Netflix is just a generation away from Blockbuster. The iPod is a close cousin of the Sony Walkman. New products that no one has ever seen before are not required, and the term "disruptive" can apply to the business model as well as a product. Once you've decided upon the product concept, it's time to consider how to wrap a business around the idea.

The next step is to write a simplified business plan. You may be asking yourself why you should bother with a business plan. Doing so forces you to consolidate your thoughts and to research your product concept. How long will it take to develop your product? Will it require outside funding? How much? Who do you need on your team? Are there competitors? How will you market and sell your product, and how big is the market? What pricing strategy will you pursue? How do you plan on providing customer support, and are there regulatory hurdles to overcome? Your plan doesn't have to be a novel, but it does require substantial thought about goals and execution. I've seen many technical people who have written their business plans later, only to find out after months or even years of effort that there were no viable business models for their products.

So you've developed a business plan. Now what? Even if you fund the company yourself, you should present this plan to those who might have insight. Studies have shown that start-ups who seek outside financial assistance have a greater chance of success—not necessarily because they received financing but because the perspectives of others who have seen numerous companies unfold is valuable. You need to develop an elevator pitch, a short commercial-like presentation on the product concept and the business strategy. Most advisors and investors will start by listening to the presentation or reading the executive summary. While a business plan has many crucial elements, at the early stages of a company product vision and credibility of the team are the most important elements of all. Above all else, the first investors are investing in the people. Much to the surprise of many first time entrepreneurs, -the business strategy often gets far more attention than the product.

Funding a company is on most entrepreneurs' minds these days. Attend any meeting of the investment community, angels or venture capital, and you'll hear how entrepreneurs should focus more on bootstrapping and not approach the investment community for funding until they have a proven product concept with customers. While many venture capital firms are heading upstream to the later rounds or becoming asset managers, some venture capitalists remain committed to providing seed rounds. As a group, angel investors provide more funding to start ups than the venture capital community. While venture capitalists tend to be concentrated in a few areas, almost every region has an angel investment group and many angels do not invest far from home. Strategic partners provide another funding avenue. Established companies will often invest in start-up companies. They may want to explore new market segments with capital efficiency or they may be looking for innovations to their existing product lines. There is always the traditional network of friends and families as well. No matter the path, locating capital is not a quick process. In the early days, the company founders spend most of their time looking for funding.

Persistence matters. Cisco Systems had to meet with 77 venture capital firms to secure its first round of funding from Sequoia and the company already had hundreds of thousands of dollars of monthly revenue. The story of Colonel Sanders and Kentucky Fried Chicken is a legendary story of perseverance. Colonel Sanders endured more than a thousand rejections before he obtained his first deal. The funding process is really a sales process and any salesperson will hear prospects say "no" more often than "yes".

A start up has the advantage of being able to adapt and change rapidly. No business plan survives confrontation with market, customers, competitors, and investors. Given the time required to develop almost any technical product or service, your original idea will rarely materialize as first envisioned. You need to listen, to keep an open mind, and to be receptive to change. This is difficult for most first time entrepreneurs to do.

Starting a company is like embarking on the adventure. It's not important to know how to get from A to Z. When starting out, you need only to know how get from A to D. The product concept may be applicable to a wide range of markets. Perhaps it could be incorporated into personal computers, cell phones, or any Internet enabled device. Maybe it could be used by consumers, enterprise and small businesses. Nonetheless, there may be the possibility of producing both software and hardware versions. This is a grand vision, as each combination would be a separate product. A start-up must focus on the most promising variant, determining how to technically develop this version and gain early adopters — this would be how to get from A to D. Getting to Z, the grand vision, may take decades and it is impossible to plan the long path at the beginning. You will learn many things along the way, and Z may no longer be the desired goal. You just have to get started and enjoy the journey.

The Investors' Perspective

The difference between a mountain and a mole-hill is your perspective.

-Al Neuharth

Investors want to make money and the sooner the better. Investors are most interested in how the start-up makes money and how the start-up plans on increasing the value of the company. Interestingly enough, most entrepreneurs focus too heavily on the product and the technology. That's great if you're giving a customer presentation, but investors aren't interested in using the product. They are concerned with the business of technology.

A start-up defines and develops a product or service based upon customer needs. Likewise, when securing funding, the start-up company itself is the product. The best time to entice investors is when the start-up achieves a milestone that significantly increases company value, not when your bank account is close to disappearing. The entrepreneur needs to build a company such that it becomes attractive to the investors; if the company is to grow up, it will need financing at some point.

Much has been written about the elevator pitch, investor call back presentations, and the series ABC's alphabet pitches. The basis for all these presentations is the Slide Deck, a standardized format for presenting a start-up to the investment community. All of these presentations are for the qualifying rounds. Winning a round is not equivalent to winning the start-up game. Winning means you can keep playing. If you lose, you may be shutting down the start-up or sitting on the sidelines for awhile.

There are many version of the Slide Deck, but they all are similar in substance. Here is a typical version.

- Company Overview — Problem, Solution, Product
- Market and Market Context Your Company Addresses
- Business Model
- Progress and Milestones
- Competition and Company's Secret Sauce
- Partners, Customers & Pipeline
- Team — Founders, Advisors, and Mentors
- Finances
- Exit Opportunity

While all of these categories are important, some are more important than others. Where should an entrepreneur focus their attention? Here's a typical weighted breakdown of how a company is evaluated for funding. Look closely at the evaluation criteria, and you'll notice that it's mostly about marketing — customer understanding, market opportunity, competition, and parts of the business model such as pricing schemes are all marketing issues.

- Team (25%)
- Customer Understanding (12.5%)
- Market Opportunity (12.5%)
- Business Model (12.5%)
- Competition (12.5%)
- Product (10%)
- Financials (10%)
- Exit Opportunity (5%)

Why is the team so important? Unlike small businesses where financing is debt and the loans are collateralized with corporate or personal assets, start-up investors receive equity for their funding. There is no recourse if the company folds and collapses. Assets are usually nil. The money is gone. Second, investors believe it is easier to change the product than to change the people.

The above criteria are the perfect storm, but they may be not enough. The human side of the equation is the biggest risk of all. There was a consumer electronics start-up founded with experience in marketing, management, product development, and even a venture capitalist turned entrepreneur. For the first few years, money was no problem. The former venture capitalist knew exactly how to close on as much as was needed. The product concept was a project that had been shut down by a Fortune 500 company, and this was the original team. The initial funding came from a Japanese consumer electronics giant. It seemed they had all the right stuff. Marketing became restless with the time taken to develop the product, so they took matters into their own hands. Marketing decided to license pieces of technology to be incorporated into the product, hoping to speed up development. However, some of the licensed technology didn't have the needed performance to make the product work as desired, and some had more performance than needed, which drove the cost well beyond consumer pricing. After four years and several product variations, the company was sold for assets at a price well below the funding obtained.

Entrepreneurs often think that investors want to hear how their proposal is conservative. Start-ups are a very risky business and it has to return far more than just buying and holding publicly traded stock. If investors wanted conservative, they'd invest in Waste Management, Apple, or Coca-Cola. If the entrepreneur is conservative on the plan, investors won't believe the team will be bold enough to develop, promote, sell, and grow the business. Investors want confidence, but not arrogance. The latter often means a non-team player, incapable of understanding the customer. Investors want passion and enthusiasm because the attitude of the sales person is the most important factor in a sale, and start-ups must sell every aspect of their business to just about everyone.

Investors do want to know that the entrepreneurs will respect their money. This is particularly true of angel investors because it is their money and they earned it the hard way—by working for it. For instance, two co-founders presented to angel investors and when one investor asked what the start-up would do if problems occurred, they flippantly replied that they'd simply get their jobs back on Wall Street. While they eventually got the funds, it didn't come from the investors at this meeting. Another start-up with three co-founders had raised $1.7 million in seed money from angels and had just closed an $8 million round from a venture capital firm. Upon closing, one of the founders expressed relief and announced he could take a vacation to the Bahamas; the VCs glared disapprovingly. Yet another start-up CEO, after raising $2 million in seed money from private investors, stated that if the start-up didn't work out…well, the investors could each afford to lose their $100,000 or more. They'd still have pretty nice lives. When it came time for another funding round, the current investors would not invest further unless the CEO stepped down. No drunk and disorderly spending allowed.

Investors often want to know the start-up's role model, a proof-point that shows a business can be built using the business model. Start-ups and entrepreneurs can aspire to be like the previous success stories in the future, but they cannot copy them today. Those companies were built under yesterday's conditions. Like any customer, investors are looking to buy that with which they are familiar or comfortable

Investors often look at how the entrepreneur approaches the funding process as an early indication of how the entrepreneur will operate the startup. Entrepreneur should view the investment community – venture capitalists, angel investment groups, super angels – as the customers in a small market, and like any other market, customers trust the opinion of other customers. The investment community is like a small town where most everyone knows everyone else. If the start-up's proposal is shopped around to most possible investors, and none elect to invest then the current and future potential investors will start to wonder why.

Investors want to be convinced of the business proposal's worthiness and be reassured that the team can make the vision a reality. While obtaining outside funding is useful, investors are not required. I have met founders of tech companies who have built companies to $500 million or close to a billion in annual sales without taking money from venture capitalists or the like. However, it does take much longer than an investor-backed start-up. Regardless of whether or not it is investor-backed, these investors' considerations are needed for all new companies to succeed.

Product

Exploring a Product Concept

Those who stay closely connected to customers and who are inspired and guided by them continue to drive their company's innovation process.

-Harry Beckwith

The product or service is the heart of any business proposition. However, investors disproportionately give the product a minority interest when they consider investing in a company. Why? As noted earlier: the product is to the start-up what the heart is to the human body, of critical importance but not the only critical element. A great product alone will not make a successful start-up, yet it all starts with the product concept.

Customers are the best resource for defining and creating a new product. Venture capitalists like to have a team with experience in the specific industry and understand that the marketing person is a vital team member from the beginning. The marketing person with experience in the specific technology has had access to the customers.

Entrepreneurs tend to make two big mistakes. The first is the entrepreneur who believes everyone is like them and if they like the product then everyone else will. Therefore: never extrapolate the market or the crowd from your own experience. Get the product into the hands of the customer as soon as possible and see whether they embrace it. The second mistake is the techie founder who focuses heavily on the technical aspects of the product—not on the customers. Start-up teams must fall in love with the market and customers, not with their product. The product meets the needs of the customers, not the other way around.

The first step to product definition is to make assumptions about the product and its bells and whistles, then find the customers. If the market space or closely related one exists today, then a market research firm somewhere is tracking these markets. Like the historical perspective of facts and dates, statistics provided by market research firms point a start-up in the right direction for customers, but they are not a replacement for speaking with them. A deep knowledge of the customer is crucial. Many entrepreneurs present the market numbers generated from research firms as evidence of customer insight and demand. Savvy investors want more. Most already know the market numbers and when they ask for the statistics, it's a filter to see if the entrepreneur has bothered with some simple research into the matter. The insights are far more valuable.

Consumers are easier to access today than ever. The Internet is primarily a consumer media and with the advent of social networking, the consumer can be directly accessed. If you want to find out what consumers think of a set of products, go to the review sites and read the most negative and positive reviews. The average review is 4.5 out of 5; in this case, ignore the numbers and read the reviews. Users will usually tell you what they loved and hated, and sometimes write what they wished was available in the product. Likewise, what are people talking about on social sites such as Twitter and Facebook, and what are they searching with their keyword? Keywords are a bit tricky. Google reported at a conference that 20% of searches conducted every day have never been done before. One third of all searches results in no click on any of the results. Thanks to the large shopping portals and comparison shopping sites, you can even determine the relative volume of sales of items from the sales rankings. Customers vote with their dollars and this is easily traceable. Customers can be accessed through online survey sites as well. The drawback is both you and your competitors have access to the same information.

Niche consumer products can find customers at events. There is a healthcare start-up that set up booths at farmer markets, wellness fairs, and sporting events such as local marathons to introduce their product and do customer research prior to the product's introduction. Business products can find their customers at trade shows and conferences as well.

Keep in mind that when defining a consumer product, consumer behavior doesn't change as quickly as we might think. Social networking has seemingly taken the world instantly by storm, but the first social networking company was funded by venture capitalists in 1997 and it failed because the market wasn't ready.

Businesses are always eager to hear about a new product or service that can help them. While the Internet has brought tremendous insight into consumers, much business to business interaction is handled as in the past. It still comes to relationships with the customers. Customers like to be acknowledged. So if you add a feature that a customer specifically requested, make sure you tell them that you added the feature for them even if another 1,000 customers asked for the same function.

Like any other part of the process, communicating with the customers happens early when you are defining the process and often continues as long as the start-up exists. While understanding the customers is of primary importance, the secondary keys to defining a new product are observation, creativity, and practical design. You may be talking to your customers early, but everyone in marketing knows that customers are not always truthful. If you haven't built a relationship with the customer, they may be guarded in what they are willing to tell you.

As you greet someone, we are programmed to ask, "How are you today?" We expect a simple response: "I'm doing fine today and how has your day been going?" We don't expect the person to launch into a lengthy analysis of what has gone wrong with their day so far. We don't expect, "My car broke down and I had to wait for the tow truck as my child was screaming in the back of the car. As my car was being towed, my neighbor called to say a fire truck was putting out a fire in my garage. And my spouse sent me a text message saying it was time for a divorce." Customers behave the same way. It takes time to get your customers to open up about what their problems are. Sometimes customers don't want to admit to their problems to the outside world. If someone takes 5 days to perform a simple task with the software, they may not want to admit to it when their boss thinks it should be a 15 minute task.

One can draw parallels between Hollywood and the high tech industry. Despite the decades of making movies and TV shows, the Hollywood studios still develop pilot series to gauge the viability of a show—and still have box office duds. People change; what was successful yesterday won't necessarily work today or tomorrow. Consumers are unpredictable. American Idol was a way of taking the selection process directly to the consumer. Likewise with high tech consumer products; we often release a stripped down version in the market to validate the product concept. Then the metrics are monitored to get a notion of product viability. Simply put, the waters are tested before jumping in.

The start-up won't be able to entirely define the product before starting the product development phase. Marketing goes on in parallel with development, and much to developers' annoyance, their designs have to change to reflect the change in customer requirements.

- work w/ legislators to get mitigation & energy
  audits included in home buyer inspections
  (& appraisals?)

The Concept Plan

The key to innovation is collective creative effort.
The key to creative effort is to collect a variety of
ideas from a diverse group of people.
— Unknown

Everyone tells an entrepreneur to write a business plan. Why? Because writing the plan forces one to think about the important aspects of the plan, to clarify one's thinking, and to plan at least a rudimentary strategy to take your business from an idea to a product. Don't dive in just yet. First, start with a concept plan, a precursor to a business plan that allows the entrepreneur to explore the concept with the customer and investors.

The concept plan is a shorter document to introduce the business to potential investors, customers, and advisors. This is an advice-only proposal. The intent is to discover. It introduces the various stakeholders into the business process early. Stakeholders are investors, customers, partners, advisors, and anyone you need to make your vision a reality. The real opportunity in the market will emerge and the successful product will evolve. The entrepreneur is searching for the right product, the right customers, and the right marketing.

Most people involved in the start-up community are verbally-oriented, so don't necessarily expect them to read the concept plan — some will, but most won't. They will expect you to speak about it. Most investors are used to reviewing executive summaries so put the concept plan into a similar format. When speaking with investors, learn what they think of the idea before asking for funding. Next, most investors have portfolio companies. Find out who those companies are, do research to see if any of those companies have any similarities with your project, and ask those investors about those companies' mistakes and accomplishments. Once you have feedback, modify your idea and business model accordingly. In the end, there are three questions you must answer before developing the more detailed business plan: Do the customers want the product (needing a must-have product is better)? Are customers willing to pay for it? Is the project fundable?

Do you want to know how you sound to people before approaching them? There are a few techniques you can use ahead of time. If you are prone to adding pauses or fillers into your speech such as uh's and um's, try recording and playing back your words. It usually takes about three times of hearing these in your own speech for a person to change. There are online aids as well such as audio and video recordings available at audioacrobat.com or products such as Camtasia Studio.

The concept plan is no longer than five pages. It has a product description: in other words, the problems solved by this product. It includes a market description—the size of the market, the number of potential customers, the current value chain and the portion of the value chain that the plan addresses and captures. You should calculate the extreme; what if you captured 100% of the market? It has the back-of-the-envelope profitability assessment —revenue and profitability. It has a resource plan—what it takes to produce this product. You may want to include a basic risk assessment. In my experience, if you can identify a risk, write a contingency plan and know how to mitigate the risk, then it's a manageable roadblock. The real start-up killers are those the entrepreneur never thought would ever happen.

Stakeholders have different perspectives. There's a difference between customer and investor presentations. The customer cares most about the product and how it improves their lives. Customers don't care about profitability or revenue projections. An investor cares about the return on investment and when the return can be expected. Once you have the concept plan, create two versions: one for the customer and one for the investor.

As a rule, you want to get the stakeholders excited about the proposals first. You don't want to lead them in their thoughts too early. You want their impressions and opinions. You want to start a dialogue, not a yes and no question-and-answer session. While you want to develop a basic risk assessment, don't include this in any version of the concept plan. Customers won't care because they want you to solve their problem; they don't care about the risks of creating the product. Investors evaluate many proposals and they look for reasons to *not* invest. If they can't find an objection, then it is potentially fundable. Even though you are asking for advice only, don't mention risks and potential hurdles at this stage; let the investor bring up the subject. Finally, when speaking with investors, ask what milestones you would need to achieve for them to consider funding.

The concept plan serves a few other purposes. As an entrepreneur, you want to validate your idea quickly and cheaply. It's better to die a quick death than to endure a slow one. There's no point in working on a project for years that won't work. At the concept stage, stakeholders are more likely than not to be polite and agree that your idea has merit. If you feel you are meeting resistance at the concept stage, don't swim upstream. It's a recipe for disaster. Modify your concept to make it more palatable to the stakeholders.

The entrepreneur should keep these stakeholders up-to-date on your progress. This update doesn't have to be a formal meeting; it could be as simple as an email or a get-together for coffee. If your project is to succeed, you are going to need these people again in the life of the company.

If you decide to proceed, write the detailed start-up business plan and an executive summary. It seems like a daunting process because most business plan guidebooks are structured for well-established, complex businesses but not all business plans are equal. Keep it simple. Find one that works for your start-up.

Concept Plan Outline

The investor concept plan is intended to introduce the company and its product from a funding perspective. It is very similar to an executive summary, but several sections may be missing. When engaging in a conversation about the concept plan, the start-up should have one to two intended goals for the conversation. Recently, I introduced a concept plan for a consumer Internet start-up to several venture capitalists. Each had portfolio companies that had similarities to the proposed company, and I had very specific information I was interested in finding out – what they thought about the business and market, what were their portfolio companies' roadblocks and challenges, and what would it take for them to invest in such a proposal.

Company Overview

- What is the purpose of the company and its vision?

- How the company would be classified, what type of product or service does it offer, and what specific market segment does it address?
- Problem Addressed or Market Opportunity
- What is the problem being addressed and what is the severity of the problem?
- What is the solution? What is its value proposition?

Start-ups imply technology. This section needs to be explained in terms that everyone can easily understand. One suggestion is to take any documentation already written, hire some freelance writers and let them create these words from this documentation. First, professional writers are simply better than most people at conveying information succinctly. You don't want to get overly involved in describing the problem and its solution, but it can't be vague and general either. Second, it will show what an everyday reader, not intimately familiar with the product, will gleam out of the longer documentation. The freelance writers can easily be hired through websites such as Elance.com.

Great idea

Market

- What is the addressable market size?
- Is it growing?
- What is the geographic location of this market?

Business Model

- How does the start-up intend to make money?
- How will the product be sold?

35

A concept plan for a customer is a variation. The description of the market and the business should be replaced by the following.

Key Product Capabilities

- What are the top features and their associated benefits?

Customer Usage

- What exactly is your product? How does the customer use it?
- Are there any significant ramifications the customer should be aware of, e.g. does it increase power usage by 10%?

The concept plan is meant to engage either a customer or investor in a discussion. Enough information should be provided to get the discussion going, but not so much that it becomes a yes or no question and answer session. You want to solicit an opinion or receive advice.

Customer
Understanding

Engaging Customers

*If you engage people on a vital, important level,
they will respond.*
—Edward Bond

Marketing starts immediately—often before the product is available to the customer. Start-ups need to demonstrate market validation and customer acceptance prior to funding. The initial marketing focuses on gaining a better understanding of customer needs, planting the seeds to build customer relationships, and beginning a pre-launch awareness program. It is not the go-to-market plan; it is a search plan. It means knowing how customers conduct their business and how the product or service can add value to their business model. It also includes knowing your customers' habits, communities, and media preferences. This feedback is critical in refining and prioritizing product features as well as gaining insight into the correct pricing. Early customer discussions will facilitate a long term relationship as they like to provide feedback and will often buy a product that meets their needs!

On day one, marketing activities often center on creating awareness, searching for customers and partners, and looking for markets. Marketing must have a buyer-centric viewpoint. The first step is to create your target customer profile and identify a list of potential customers. While this seems simple, it is done incorrectly—or not at all. Sometimes your assumed target audience doesn't want your product; you end up changing the customer definition and maybe the product definition as well. There also may be a difference between who the end user is and who your customer is. Just look at Google. The audience is consumers searching for Internet content and customers are the advertisers. The customer pays for the product or service.

Start with a brainstorming session with who can use your product and where these users, customers, or audience can be found. Typically, a start-up's notion of their customer is refined after they start talking to these customers.

Some Search Techniques for Finding the Customer

It's amazing what you can determine about a company from a group of job postings, and the job boards have convenient multi-faceted search filters. Many companies don't like to divulge future plans publicly, but they will detail plans in job descriptions to attract the best talent. Every company, from start-up to Fortune 500, is on a job board somewhere. You can also do a lot of company research by reading the job postings.

Trade shows, conferences, and workshops are a great way to find companies interested in a technology or market. Attendees all have a targeted interest. Attendees are busy and sometimes don't have the time to talk. I have been scheduled in meetings from 8 A.M. to 8 P.M. at large trade show events. Consider the size of the venue. Some trade shows have tens of thousands of attendees, and spare time is scarce. You may be able to get far more information from events that have only a few hundred attendees. Instead of trying to corner people at the tradeshow, contact them in advance and arrange a time to speak. For smaller events, you may be able to buy the attendee list or even buy the previous year's attendance list. Even with consumer products, consumers still congregate at certain events.

Through technical conferences or standard meetings, you can find out who's in charge of a project group. While sales and marketing people may be wary of turning over the names and contact information of internal people, technical folks are usually much more willing to help find the right person in their organization. Also, finding the technical person through a byline on a technical article can eventually lead one to the person you want to speak with.

Another method is to create a topical website with advice and information about the topic area where your product or service will be applied. Why advice? Because authors of successful e-books know that advice outsells information. Likewise, Ann Landers' newspaper column was successful because she offered specific advice about readers' problems. Therefore, advice is of primary concern. Information is also important but will be of secondary concern. What do people do when they search for an answer to a problem? They Google it. It's amazing how interested people will subscribe to a free email list. You can use the email list to contact subscribers and ask to set up a brief phone call with them to discuss how you can better address their concerns in your newsletter. In my experience, those actively seeking answers to immediate problems respond, and you'll get about a 10% response rate. You can send an email survey to the others.

Marketing builds awareness for your product or service. Talking to potential customers early in the development process ensures they are integrated early into a feedback and eventual beta program. Sales rules still apply: customers buy what is the most familiar and it takes at least 7 contacts for a purchase to be considered.

Getting the Customer to Speak with You

You found your customers; you know who and where they are, but how do you get the customers to talk with you about their needs and problems? How can you gauge their reception to the product under development? Getting potential customers to speak with you is not always easy, and building a relationship doesn't happen overnight. Even if customers speak with you, they are often guarded until they know you. And yet, customers don't always tell the truth either. So what do you do?

If you haven't yet done marketing or sales, you need to be aware that this is a time consuming process. If you are doing marketing in a start-up, don't think you can do it along with another task. Marketing is a full time challenge, even before the product is available. Start-up survival depends on marketing efforts. This is a big mistake at many start-ups: believing product development comes first and marketing can be done later—and less strenuously. As Mark Twain said, "Thousands of geniuses live and die undiscovered." The same holds true for start-up companies; most flare up and flame out before anyone knew they ever existed. Most stumble in marketing and sales, not in technology.

Voice mail can be your best ally in this effort. Most people call a potential customer and if they don't pick up, they leave a message. Imagine that you leave a message such as, "This is John Doe from XYZ Company and we are developing a new widget. Call me back at your convenience at (123) 555-4141." Most likely it'll be deleted. Most marketing folks will call back again. They get asked to leave another message, and they leave the same message—except this time, the listener deletes the message before it ends. If you keep leaving them, the sooner and sooner the listener will delete the message, and the listener will hope you'll just go away. If you leave a message enough times, the listener may call you back out of annoyance—and with no intention of discussing your ideas. You're clogging up their voice mailbox. Now what?

A more systematic approach is a voice mail campaign. Brainstorm about why your potential customer would want to spend their time helping your create a new product. At this point, you haven't talked to your customers so you are making assumptions. Write down 24 short statements about how your new product can benefit them or solve a problem for them. Then prioritize these messages. The next time you call and get voice mail, leave one of these messages and every time you call again, leave another. Now you are building a story. Not all customers will need your product for the same reasons. Keep track of which message eventually gets the customer to return your call. A typical voice mail campaign would have the caller leave 2 messages per week for the first two weeks, 1 message per week for the next four weeks, and finally 1 message per month for the next four months. If your customer is interested, 5 to 8 message are usually needed to inspire a return call. Customers are much more receptive to cold calls at work than at home. After all, their employers are paying for them to listen to you.

Email is overused. If you use email, the subject line is critical. Most readers never open the email. They elect to delete or read it based upon the subject line. The subject should be compelling. Use your best tidbit because readers will assume there is even more valuable information inside the email. Even if the reader opens the email, you have only the first few sentences to attract their attention and keep them reading to the call to action request — schedule a meeting or phone conversation.

The explosion of email has made snail mail more effective. Recipients will read a physical letter these days because they are rare. Express mail is even better, particularly if you are trying to connect with a person in a larger organization. Internal mailrooms can be slow in delivering snail mail to addressees and often they can sit in a mail slot for some time before being picked up, but express mail is quickly delivered.

Cornering a potential customer at an event is another way to get them to speak with you. Smaller events are better. The restroom marketing approach is a clever way to meet your potential customers. Here's how a B2B enterprise software start-up did it. The marketing person bought the list of attendees for a small conference prior to the event date. He cross referenced the list to their potential customers, memorized the list of names, and staked out the restroom area at the conference. As people left the restrooms, he noted the name on their conference name tags, and approached those on his target list. The marketing person knew the person would have at least a few minutes to speak with him as the customer was walking from the restroom area back to the conference area where the programs were being held. In fact, this is how he first met their first big customer.

Are your potential customers speaking at an event? Most senior managers speak at industry events. If you're local, many will speak at community events as well. After your potential customer speaks, introduce yourself. Many times, simply greeting someone creates a personal connection. Calling them within 48 hours of the introduction often gets you a meeting. If it seems that many people want to talk with the speaker afterwards, speakers are usually free just before a presentation.

Most startups are cash strapped and don't have a lot of funds to spend on numerous conferences, tradeshows, and program meetings, but they need to seek out the connections attending these events. One way is to volunteer to work at these events

— some startups may even ask to register the speakers and panelists. As a volunteer, you get access to information about attendees and you will get full access to the events. This is useful for events that are closed or have requirements regarding who can attend.

Before you jump into a full blown product development and marketing effort, be sure that the problem is real and customers desire an answer. Start-ups need a strong understanding of customer needs and problems. Otherwise, entrepreneurs may end up with a product in search of a problem.

Knowing Customers

*You'll find the key insights you need — after your
own, which are the most critical — in the minds
key market observers and prospects. But they do
not readily volunteer those insights.*
— Harry Beckwith

Beginning a start-up requires the ideal balance of what a customer wants and is willing to pay for, what a start-up can create in a reasonable amount of time and budget, at what price the start-up can offer the product to the customer, and what product can capture enough market share to make a sustainable business. Marketing is the first stumbling block. If the start-up is a software company, there is little doubt the software package can be defined, coded, compiled, tested, documented, and offered for sale, but whether customers will buy and use the software is far more uncertain. Understanding the customer is the key to market acceptance.

Customers do not view the product in the start-up's business terms. Customers care about what's in it for them, not for the start-up. They are the human side of product development: sometimes unpredictable, irrational, and emotional. While this seems to be obvious when referring to consumers, it is true for businesses as well. Despite the empirical evaluation of the purchase, the decision maker, the champion of the product, and the business users are all humans.

CAUTION: Early Adopters Are Not Mainstream Customers

Customers are not created equal. It seems obvious, but the danger lies in assuming the first customers are the same as the majority of customers, and letting the euphoria of winning those early customers become a belief that the product will be successful. Early adopters are risk-takers, enthusiastic and sometimes visionary. They want the latest electronic gadgets and enjoy showing off their new toys. They will accept a feature-limited, not-so-easy-to-use version to gain some advantage. They are willing to pay a higher introductory price. They are usually the ones with an immediate problem that needed to be solved yesterday and desperate for a solution. Early adopters will spread the word about the product. These early adopters are less than 10% of the potential customers. Conversely, mainstream customers are practical. They want tested, proven, full-featured, easy-to-use technology at a reasonable price. They are also pragmatists. The start-up needs them because they will be the bulk of the revenue. Late adopters are reluctant and risk averse. They have to be dragged, kicking and screaming, into the new era. Left with no choice but to change, they will grudgingly try the new-fangled device. Late adopters are less than 10% of the potential customer base. Many start-ups have failed because they didn't realize the difference between the early adopters and the mainstream customers. The mainstreamers make the difference between an operating loss and a profit.

What causes the failure when companies can't distinguish between early adopters and mainstreamers? The first failure occurs when the company engages in expensive advertising and promotion after these early adopters have seemingly validated the demand for the product. When the sales leads don't materialize, what's the reaction? Sales is considered to be the problem because they aren't closing enough deals on those few precious leads, and new sales people are employed to correct the incompetence with the current sales force. Next, marketing is blamed for not generating enough demand. The solution is to create better ads and engage the customer on different or more channels. The burn rate at the company sky rockets, and there are still scant sales. The second failure is believing that customers attracted to free products are indicative of paying customers. One of the dot-com lessons is that there is unlimited demand for free products. Discount shoppers rarely pay full price; they just look for the next supplier willing to offer them the best discount. If there are multiple providers, a race to the bottom can break out. If a marketing and sales strategy is based on what's important to a free customer, the start-up may never attract the paying customers. Today, unless your product is targeted at creating a new market space, giving away a product to build market share is viewed as absence of a marketing and sales plan—a "we'll figure it out later" strategy.

CAUTION: Customers Don't Always Tell the Truth

I was at a sporting competition for children the other day. Every time one of the kids did something, as a parent I dutifully cheered and encouraged them with words of "good job," regardless of whether it was a disastrous maneuver or not. Customers behave similarly. Customers don't always tell us the truth, but they're not really liars. They spare our feelings. Often customers dislike bearing bad news or they may be non-confrontational or they may engage in wishful thinking. As J.P.

Morgan said many decades ago, "A man always has two reasons for doing anything — a good reason and the real reason."

I was in a customer meeting with a software company that was just turning seven years old. The founder and CEO had come to ask his biggest customer for feedback on the company's flagship product. The audience gave glowing reviews of the software, and when he mentioned possible new features or future products, the audience was enthusiastic. As the audience exited, small groups muttered about the difficulty of the current features and how they'd never use many of the proposed ones. What happened? His biggest customer was an old, established giant of a company, where skills in office politics—more than performance—determine one's career path. Employees learned that in order to thrive, they had to be publicly upbeat, and this behavior was applied to the customer meeting. The CEO of the software company wanted blunt feedback—the good, the bad, and the ugly—but he got only sugar coating.

One way to circumvent the above behavior is to watch your customers' behaviors and ignore their words. Send someone into your customers' offices and have them show you how they are using your product or ask to observe as they are using it. The truth of your product will be revealed. That's not to say that they will accurately show you what they do because simply being observed may cause them to behave differently. But with technology, if the customer can't find the right series of clicks, your product isn't being used as you intend. Excel is a commonly used spreadsheet program that allows users to analyze and manipulate data. It's amazing the number people I've seen use Excel to format documents like a word processor because they don't know how to use Word.

Talking to your customers regularly will enable them to speak more freely. You will often glean more information from the side comments and one-liners than responses to direct questions. Talking to your customers out of the blue puts your customers on their guard. Imagine someone you haven't seen in 10 years calling you and asking to borrow money. Are you going to loan it to them? Not likely, but if they are someone you see regularly, you might. It's a good idea to keep your customers talking. In fact, it has been determined that it takes about 20 minutes of interacting with another person before a person become comfortable to speak somewhat openly.

CAUTION: When Customers Tell You What They Want, It's Limited, Not Visionary

If you ask customers what they would like changed in a product, what will they say? First, they will ask you to provide functions they find missing or to fix what does not work well. They will ask for an incremental improvement in what is currently available. Second, they will ask for features that the competitors offer. And if customers look beyond your competitors' products, they will look to unrelated products and ask to transfer features in these products to yours. This is how products from different companies consolidate into a common set of features. Just think about your car, is it really different than the dozens of others in the marketplace? The question a start-up has to answer is whether or not one can truly differentiate its product in the minds of the customers by offering slight improvements over the existing product.

So if you want to offer a revolutionary product, one that is truly unique, you won't get that information from the customer. We have all heard someone say to us, "I don't know what I want, but if I see it, I'll know it's what I'm looking for." The customer may describe the problems, but the vision of how to solve that problem must come from the start-up. A customer can be shown a mock-up or demo and, from the tangible, offer suggestions. The saying "If a picture is worth a thousand words then a demo is with a million" is very true. If a demo isn't possible, then it becomes a matter of creating a familiar way for customers to visualize the product: a metaphor can make a revolutionary product more tangible.

Start-ups can conduct online surveys and focus groups using services from Survey Monkey, Zoomerang, and Survey Gizmo, to name a few. However, I have found that the more niche a product or service, the less likely an online survey service can find the right participants. Don't expect a great return on the number of surveys—even on Amazon only about 10% of buyers provide the ratings. Alternatively, blogging about the topic, particularly about the problems, can elicit comments from those experiencing them. To learn the basic of blogging, sites such as problogger.net, copyblogger.com or how tomakemyblog.com are great references.

Business customers are easier to access directly than less approachable mass market consumers. Start-ups can conduct surveys and interviews with consumers, but relatively few can be contacted. Potential partners are companies or organizations with existing customer or membership bases representative of your potential customers: not only might you access the consumer through them, but they might be able to offer insight into these customers. Partners also may be channel partners or distributors. In addition, industry experts, analysts, or influencers may have insight into your intended customers or may hold opinions respected by your buyers. Investors have seen a lot, and while they might not be able to provide direct knowledge of the customer, they have seen how other companies have operated and know what has worked and what hasn't. The goal is to be an outside-looking company to create a product based on customer needs and to determine how your start-up can attract these customers later, when the product is ready to ship.

Finding and accessing customers isn't easy. Once you can interact, understanding customers is not necessarily straight-forward. While statistics and numbers provided by market analysts may point a start-up in the right direction, nothing replaces speaking with the customers.

Customers' Common Sense Concerns

If you give them something worth paying for, they'll pay. Treat the customer as an appreciating asset.
—Tom Peters

Enticing customers with the product idea is difficult. Getting customers to pay is even harder. Who wants to do business with an unknown? No one. Will a customer do business with nobody? Yes, but only if they have no other choice, or the risk is minimal and the benefit is great.

A start-up making a new networking component had a meeting with a potential customer. A few decades ago, the prospect was also a start-up, and now it was a multi-national, Fortune 1000 company. The start-up worked hard and the customer needed its new system design. The Fortune 1000 company showed great interest. Enthusiasm built in the start-up as the prospect continued delving into the new technology and the relationship seemed promising. The start-up delivered a lengthy detailed specification of the component in PDF format to the Fortune 1000 company. They were impressed. One day the Fortune 1000 company called and asked if they could have the Microsoft Word version of the specification. Why? They want to use it as a base to develop their own proposal to circulate among their trusted suppliers to see if one of them will produce the part for them. What happened? They didn't want to risk the ship date of their system on an unknown start-up. They needed the component, but desired a more reliable source. The prospect could have considered acquiring the start-up, but that was costly. Why not see if one of the established suppliers would do it? Get the component and avoid the acquisition costs.

I have often encountered this situation. The prospects who need and want the product will approach their suppliers; plant the seeds about developing a similar product and mention they would like to buy soon. Many entrepreneurs believe that a non-disclosure agreement (NDA) will prevent their information from circulating. Large corporations know a start-up does not have the deep financial pockets to pursue a breach of a NDA and time is on the side of the established player. Stealth mode is a myth. If a start-up talks with customers and investors, word gets around quickly.

From the customer's perspective, a start-up is risky. If the start-up's product is not ready today, what is the likelihood the start-up can deliver? The start-up may lack a customer service group and therefore how will the fledgling provide customer support? Will the start-up remain in business? Which investors are financing them now? In a customer's mind, the more prestigious a start-up's investors and the more money raised, the more likely the start-up will prosper. Does the start-up have a roadmap? The prospect may be producing a product family and need variations to meet the requirements of the additional products. Can the start-up develop these variations? If the start-up collapses, can the prospect recover quickly for the loss? What happens if the start-up is acquired by a competitor? What will happen to their product line? Bootstrapped start-ups make potential customers wearier than investor-backed ones. Even the number of people involved in a start-up raises concerns with customers; the smaller the start-up and the fewer full time employees, the greater the unease. Whenever a start-up produces a technology that will affect the revenue stream of the prospect, such concerns are inevitable.

So what's a start-up to do? The easier it is for the prospect to recover from the collapse of the start-up the better. The shorter the time to receiving the benefit with no follow-on obligation, the less risky the transaction to the customer, e.g. integrating new financial database software into your company is a long-term, important decision, whereas buying a cup of coffee at the latest coffee house is not. The more of the total end solution the start-up provides, the better. The closer the start-up is to the corporate life stage of the prospect, the less nervous the prospect will be.

One way to calm customers is to sell products through a reference sale program of a large corporation. Customers often feel the start-up product is now backed by the larger company and if the start-up collapses, the larger company will assume responsibility for the start-up's product.

Start-ups should find initial customers willing to endorse the product, offer testimonials for future customers, and provide references for investors. It's not just about providing a user opinion about the technology; it's also about the responsiveness of customer service, the timeliness of the deliveries, and the like.

Many entrepreneurs have difficulty seeing beyond the direct benefits of the technology to realize their customers have many commonsense concerns.

Market Opportunity

What is Marketing and How Important Is It?

"The aim of marketing is to know and understand the customer so well the product or service fits him and sells itself."

-Peter F. Drucker

Today's investors are not interested in funding start-ups that don't know how, where, and to whom to sell. What is marketing and how does it relate to business development and sales? Marketing is not sales. Marketing tells people about your product, service, and company early and often. Marketing generates demand and sales leads.

Because everyone has been exposed to marketing efforts, many entrepreneurs have a mistaken sense of what marketing is and when it is started from a consumer's perspective. This mistake often causes a common misstep in start-ups, which is only compounded by the idea of a stealth mode start-up and the need to maintain secrecy. The result: the start-up doesn't interact with customers before the product is ready, and the product definition, pre-launch awareness and initial lead generation all suffer. A start-up once asked me to mediate a dispute between their system architect and their marketing person over the features needed in the product. They were defining the product without the customer. I declined and over a year later, the CEO contacted me and asked if I would rework the product definition. The start-up had released the product to the marketplace and their target customers told them they had missed many of their basic functional requirements.

Marketing and business development must start before any sales efforts. Business development identifies new markets and develops partnerships. Sales teams reach out to those leads and convert them into paying customers. A vague plan for marketing will fail. I've heard many marketing plans with no more details than common terminology of going viral, using social networking, and offering free trials—and those clichés were the extent of the marketing strategy. Would you buy a house sight unseen from the listing description of it — 4 bedrooms, 3 baths, 2-car garage, colonial on a large lot? Would an investor fund a company with little notion of how to attract paying customers?

Marketing is neither free nor inexpensive. The right marketing plan should be a significant part of the budget for a start up and should be included in any discussion about funding and revenue. Sales and marketing expenses of publically traded companies are typically 1.5 to 2 times research and development expenses. It's rare for a start-up to fail because the company couldn't develop the technology. Investors often consider marketing and sales to be the first major stumbling point. If you need a new car, as a potential buyer you want to know the price, features, and performance of the vehicle. But if you are looking to buy stock in the car company, the car models have little weight in deciding whether you will become a shareholder.

In a start-up, there are two distinctive marketing efforts. The first is focused on the product or service. This is the product marketing and corporate branding process. A second is centered on investors and funding, where the start up itself is the product offering. These are interconnected activities. Every promotion builds awareness in the marketplace and also in the investment community. Evaluation of a company from an early stage investment perspective can put marketing at 50% of the funding decision. Continuation of funding in future rounds may require the achievement of marketing milestones.

Early marketing strategies often center on creating awareness and lead generation. Creating product and company awareness before, during, and after the development process ensures the sales and revenue plans can be attained. These relationships and leads enable the sales team to make deals and capture revenue after the product is available. People buy what's familiar. Depending on the product or service, marketing efforts can start up to 12 months before the product is available to the market for purchase.

All products solve a problem for someone. The first step in answering these questions is to identify those who most need to solve this problem. Focus on customers who *must* have the product. The second step is to find as many places as possible to access these customers and build awareness. Marketing requires planning and execution discipline—prioritizing the approaches, exploring new avenues to reach the market, tracking progress, and so on.

The marketing plan does not need to be a lengthy document that takes a year to devise, but there does need to be some semblance of what needs to be done and when. Early on, the marketing plan is a flexible document because changes are inevitable. Initially, a start-up needs to identify customers then learn how to translate that customer base into a viable business. How do you promote the company and product to that customer? How do you price the product and create value for the customer?

The marketing plan, like every aspect of a business plan, is based on assumptions. Reaching out to the customers is vital because a start-up needs to test assumptions as soon as possible. Before jumping into a full blown product development and marketing effort, you must know that the problem is *real* and customers are urgently seeking a solution.

A common start-up error occurs when the technical founder attempts both product development and marketing. It doesn't work. The technical developer is usually an introvert who prefers to be in the office hacking code or tinkering with the mechanics. The marketing person is an extrovert who wants to be out of the office talking to people and searching for new opportunities and deals. Finding a strong technologist and marketer in the same person is as likely as a Nobel Prize winning scientist winning an Olympic gold medal.

A consequence of start-ups being on shoestring budget is that the marketing and initial sales effort often fall to a single person. A start-up needs a seasoned marketing person. But a good, experienced marketing person knows that investors consider marketing the first big hurdle and won't join a start-up unless they know they can succeed with the product. They don't want to be a scapegoat and they don't want a failure on their resume.

A second common mistake occurs when a start-up realizes they need a marketing plan to get funded or they need to respond to pressure from their investors so they hire a marketing consultant to write THE PLAN. But they don't hire anyone to execute the plan. Times passes and they eventually hire the first marketing person. Now, the investors may be holding the start-up accountable for the milestones established in the marketing plan. The new marketing person may want to modify or completely re-do the plan. Furthermore, how can product development create the right product for the customers without feedback from the customers? The start-up is in a quagmire.

Marketing interacts with customers to prep the market for the product before development is completed. Marketing *cannot* be an afterthought. Investors want a founding start-up team to include both technical development and marketing. Ultimately, what the customer needs and is willing to pay for rules a start-up; marketing is the spyglass into the customer's perspective.

Creating the Marketing Strategy

There is only one valid definition of business
purpose: to create a customer
—Peter Drucker

A start-up is always cash strapped, more so today than in previous years when the capital markets were booming. A start-up also has time constraints; they can't spend a long time defining a marketing process and writing a plan. Don't get me wrong: you need a plan…but not one equivalent to the US tax code. A marketing plan appropriate for a large, established player is not suitable for a start-up. Most large companies have a formalized marketing process culminating as a detailed marketing document reaching hundreds of pages. Most established companies pass their plans from one product group to another, each group modifying the plan for their specifics and expanding it with every revision. Those marketing plans weren't written overnight or in a week or for one product. One of the hardest aspects of a marketing plan is waiting, knowing when the plan is not ready for implementation, and getting the resources and budget lined up. Most people want to jump in and get going. Ask yourself this — would you start building a house before you had a blueprint, when all you had was a vague vision in your mind of what you wanted? Even if you had a blueprint and a general contractor, wouldn't you ask for benchmarks to gauge the contractor's progress?

An established player can start the marketing effort much later in a product cycle than a start-up. They have a presence in the market, industry clout, an established customer base, distribution channels, a large group of workers dedicated to marketing, and the budget to implement a simultaneous, multi-pronged approach. Start-ups have none of these—and sometimes not even the workers. A well funded start-up might have one or two people dedicated to marketing, sales and business development with other staff members joining the effort on a part time basis.

To devise a marketing plan, you first need a marketing person. Most early stage start-ups only have a sole marketing person and this makes the choice of the marketing person critical. Find a seasoned marketing person early, develop a plan, and get going on it. It's not easy being the one person show and to build a market presence from nothing. It is difficult to find a marketing person who understands marketing communications: awareness creation such as PR, launch requirements, tradeshows and branding as well as expertise in creating leads for new customers or partners. A common misstep is to look for an experienced person from a major industry player. In a large company, job functions are highly compartmentalized, the roles are more task-oriented instead of creating a big picture strategy, and far more about incremental improvements than building.

Time and time again, start-ups hire a marketing person who worked for a top tier company, only to hear the marketing person express surprise that that none of their former contacts return phone calls. This is when someone truly understands the power of branding. Everyone wants to conduct business with an industry's top players or the Fortune 500 companies. Few companies are willing to conduct business with a start-up that has yet to make its mark.

What are the elements of a marketing effort? Most often one hears the terms *marketing plan*, *marketing strategy*, *marketing mix* and *marketing launch*. It comes down to answering the questions: what, why, where, when, and how. A marketing plan includes the objectives, description of the customer, description of the competitors, description of the product or service, action plan and market launch including budgets and resources required, pricing, and progress tracking. The marketing mix is the often-heard acronyms of 4P's, 7P's, and 4C's. The most common is the 4P's: Place, Promotion, Product and Price and sometimes Packaging. The 7P's is an extension of the supply-side 4P's model with the addition of People, Physical Environment, and Process. The 4C's twists the supply side model into the consumer model of Commodity, Cost, Channels, Communications, and sometimes Convenience. This boils down to defining what your product is, the value proposition or reason to buy the product, how the customer learns about the product, and what indirect aspects will entice customers. An example of an indirect aspect (i.e. Physical Environment) is Trader Joe's specialty supermarkets, which uses an island theme in their stores because when people are on vacation they are more willing to try new foods. Since Trader Joe's does not always carry the same inventory, the limited time further entices customers to buy with a sense of urgency. Another example is ease of payment (i.e. Process); one of the prime reasons for shopping cart abandonment with on-line shopping is requiring the customer to set up an account to buy online. Some secondary aspects can be demonstrated with business-to-business customers, who consider more than a lower price in their purchase decisions; such considerations include suppliers' track record of on-time delivery, warranties, and customer service.

The initial marketing effort focuses on gaining a better understanding of the customers and their needs, building customer relationships, and beginning a pre-launch awareness program. It is not the go-to-market plan; it is a search plan. Initially, marketing takes place during the development process. A start-up investigates target customers and potential market segments. You may speak with customers in a market segment that may not be pursued at all. Recently, I spoke with a start-up that had a new technology for industrial water filtration. The obvious customer was municipal water treatment facilities, but the start-up quickly realized that only a few desperate municipalities would be interested in an untested, unproven technology. However, the mining and oil & gas industries were immensely interested because of the large cost savings this technology would bring to on-site water cleansing.

There is a healthcare start-up that offers medical testing directly to individuals; the testing reveals if the individual is susceptible to certain diseases. Individual weren't buying this service, at least not in numbers sufficient to make the business viable. However, physicians found the results useful and therefore were willing to ask their patients to have this service performed. Their target audience changed, so the marketing and sales plan had to be revamped. Interesting enough, I spoke with newly founded second start-up several months after the first had shifted their marketing strategy away from direct marketing to consumers. They too were using this approach. This second start-up did not realize they were copying a failed strategy.

Since start-ups must focus on some niche markets, initially marketing is a search for which set of customers and which segments are the best prospects. It's important to answer the following questions and to build a compelling story line. Why would a customer buy the product? Why wouldn't a customer simply continue doing what they do today? Why would a customer buy from your start-up instead of a competitor? What creates the urgency among your customers to buy now and not wait? The two biggest competitors are continuing a "business as usual" approach, in which case, you have to give the customer an irresistible reason to change, and in-house development or the DIY approach. Sometime the answers are not obvious. It's easy to see how a customer value proposition fits with why a customer would buy a product; it's cheaper or more effective. But some products just don't have an empirical value proposition. What's the value proposition for a music download? How do you place a value on the pleasure of a song? Even if one has the best answers to these questions, it doesn't make it a good market if there's not enough volume to produce a profit.

A start-ups search must also consider volume of customers, cost of marketing and selling, and the best potential performance ratio in terms of sales conversion. The 80/20 rule applies to most everything, and marketing is no exception. It needs to concentrate on the 80% of profit and 80% of the volume that will come from 20% of the customers or 20% of the product offering. Websites offering Freemium and pay-for-premium subscription models often have only 10% of their customer base paying the premium. Bookstores make 80% of their profit from a small handful of titles.

Marketing Launch and Action Plan

As I've stressed, a vague marketing plan will fail. The plan must use multiple channels to get your message across to your customers, usually during a phased approach. Building pre-launch awareness for the product doesn't require you to reveal your company's solution; you can engage the audience by talking about the problem and showcasing use cases that demonstrate the severity and specifics of the problem. News releases, articles in industry publications, blogs, tradeshows, conferences, and speaking engagements are low cost, simple ways to gain exposure. Later, marketing may include advertising, branding, public relations, direct selling, and opening offers—and just about any way you can attract and engage customers.

Knowing your customer is more than determining what product they need; it also means knowing how they conduct their business and how your product or service can add value to their business model. It also includes knowing your customers' habits and media preferences. This helps you understand your customers as an audience before embarking into any program — what radio stations they listen to, what websites they visit regularly, what magazines they read, which analysts they respect, which trade shows they attend, what sports they like, and so on. This detailed understanding helps you find the communication channels relevant to your customer. The goal is to spend your marketing budget as effectively as possible.

You don't want a generic target customer such as "a married woman". Be more specific— your customer is a married woman who is the Chief Purchasing Officer for the household, who has children that play soccer and tennis, who has an income of $100,000 or more, and who takes at least one family vacation a year.

Pre-launch Awareness

It is never too early to start the pre-launch awareness. It takes much longer and much more focus to perform marketing when you are completely unknown. Don't try to go head-to-head with the major players. As in Internet marketing, you want to start with the long tail search keywords, not the more generic single words. A short generic search would be "Boston travel", whereas a long tail would be "historical reenactment tourist village near Boston". It's better to dominate a specific customer segment, a niche, or a local market segment. YELP, a consumer review website, has succeeded where other similar and earlier-to-market companies failed. Much of YELP's success is attributed to first building a tremendously strong local presence in geographic areas, and then expanding into other regions.

One start-up is making software to help advertising agencies run their businesses more effectively. This software takes a labor intensive, time consuming process with plenty of middle men and reduces the cycle time and eliminates the middle men. It addresses a previously unaddressed market segment and every advertising agency can benefit from this software. They started with building a customer base locally because it gave them easier access to customers and they were able to get feedback quickly and effectively. It's a lot easier to SEE how customers are using your FREE beta software and understand what features they use more often when you can WALK INTO their offices on a regular basis. Once they establish a foothold in the local market, they plan on expanding into other cities.

One purpose of pre-launch marketing is to support the sales effort later. People buy what's familiar. Even if your competitor has a superior product, customers still tend to buy from those they know. Consumers are price sensitive and buy more on emotion, while businesses buy on empirical analysis that includes many subjective criteria and personal gain for the product's champion. Psychologists have shown that while people believe they weigh the facts and options and then make a decision, they usually make an intuitive decision then justify it later with the facts and options. The pre-launch strategy needs to build that familiarity with your product and company prior to the product's availability.

Building awareness needs to be done using multiple channels — tradeshows, conferences, standards organizations, press releases, sponsorships, speaking events, moderating meeting sessions, news organizations and reporters, Internet based approaches and so on.

While you can read about companies using Twitter and social networking to sell their products, it is not truly free because it is time consuming. Creating an Internet marketing plan that includes social media and Search Engine Optimization (SEO) tactics takes time and money to execute properly. Developing an on-line community and branding a company online cannot be done overnight. It needs to be a well orchestrated process and is also much slower than most people envision. And while some YouTube videos have gone viral, those are the rare exception. Many of those wildly popular videos produced by established companies as humorous advertisements have not increased sales.

News releases are a great way to build pre-launch awareness. Generating new releases bypasses the search engine filters for unique content. News is meant to be duplicated and thus, it is not de-valued for its non-uniqueness. In addition to content, a news release needs to answer the five questions: who, what, where, when, and why. An essential for today's web savvy customers is to include a link back to your website. Other than the obvious product and company announcements, news releases can be case studies, interviews, contest announcements, human interest, and community service. You do *not* have to have an available product to start producing new releases. After a product launch, it is a good idea to keep up the press releases for a 52 week long strategy even if they are about trivial company or product news. This stops the boost from a product launch from quickly fading and is known as a Rolling Thunder strategy. Press releases can be easily and cheaply released on the Internet through online services such as PRLog.org, PR.com and PRWeb.com.

Press releases announcing the availability of a product in the near future can gauge demand for the product. I know a fabless semiconductor company that does this, fully aware that the product won't be available in the near future. In fact, they are in the very early stages of the project. If people inquire about the product, then they know there is a demand and this is used to determine the project's funding.

Blogging on the subject area does not require the product to be currently available. You can engage with the customer by talking about the problems that your product or service will solve without talking about your solution. Find specific use cases that demonstrate the problem, thereby illustrating the need for your company's upcoming solution. Setup a free email newsletter list. It's amazing how interested people will subscribe to a free email list if they think you can help them with their problems. You can use the email list to contact subscribers via phone and learn about their problems and challenges. I do this now with a niche topic and about 20 people a week subscribe to the newsletter. Based upon some basic information they provide, I contact about half every week and ask for a follow-up phone conversations. The majority will speak with me. Why would they do this? Because I'm not trying to sell them something; I'm trying to get a better understanding of their problems so I can help them.

Write guest posts for other blogs, comment on relevant blog posts, write articles, write an e-book, speak at conferences and events, open a Twitter account and share information that illustrates your point of view. There's no end of ways to get your message out there. What forums or organizations do your potential customers participate in? What blogs and newsletters do they read? Get your message in front of them in the places where they already are.

Writing and publishing articles about your topic boosts your visibility. Many trade or professional organization publish articles of interest to their members in newsletters or journals. You can also register your articles at findarticles.com, selfgrowth.com, and ezinearticles.com.

Marketing directly to a consumer takes a long time. It's much easier to build a customer base if you piggyback on other organizations. Instead of trying to reach the customer directly, try building a relationship with another company that has an established customer base.

Is The Price Right?

Price is often the excuse for why you lost, but
rarely the reason. Look deeper. Most people who
can afford the low price have the resources to pay
far more. Your problem is not your pricing; it was
your selling. Don't charge less. Sell better.
—Harry Beckwith

If you are fortunate enough to be the advent of a technical product, one that no one has ever seen before, then you are fortunate enough to be the one who establishes the pricing structure. If not, then you must evaluate the current pricing structure for the market. There is an implied price the customer is willing to pay — and the competitors have already established entry, mainstream and premium price ranges. In the minds of the customers, pricing is the top concern even if it is free and is one of the keys to a successful product.

Pricing is partially an art: free, low-cost, Tiffany, Freemium, bundled packaging, a la carte. All companies need revenue; it allows them to maintain operations, and pricing is the way the customer votes on the worthiness of the product and the company. It's the scoreboard. If a start-up doesn't rack up enough points on the field, it loses — the product and company vanish. There are no hard and fast rules, and this makes it difficult to get pricing right—and easy to get pricing wrong. Most start-ups think little about pricing because they know it can always be changed and changed yet again later. While pricing is easy to change—after all, you merely modify some text on a piece of paper or website—not getting it right can drive customers away. Many start-ups know this and so they offer their products for free!

But free can be problematic. Most consider this option because they want to demonstrate customer acceptance of the product itself, build market share, and remove pricing as a barrier. The plan is always to charge at a later date, or to charge for additional services or add-on features. When offering their product for free, start-ups must consider their objectives and know if their goals can be achieved in other ways.

Free may get someone to try something; it is not likely to get them to pay in the future. The free sample is given to entice customers when there aren't compelling reasons for the customers to change. Consider the free samples of food in the supermarket. How many people would buy a different loaf of bread other than the one they are used to? Not many. When it comes to staples, people tend to buy the familiar—and to buy it week after week. Customers of other products are no different. When a customer uses a software product and it no longer meets their needs, what is the customer's first response? They contact the software provider and ask if an upgrade will be available soon that will meet their new needs. Customers tend to wait for the new release instead of searching for a new product offered by a different company. Once customers are familiar with a product, they resist change even if the product is awkward to use or lacks the desired performance. The current solution will have to be perceived as a roadblock before a new one will be sought. There is effort in searching for a new product, there is effort in getting a supplier approved in a corporation, there is effort in getting the budget approved, and there are career risks in introducing a new product into your company — what if it turns out to be a bigger headache than the current solution? There's also effort in training the workers to use the new product. These are some of the hidden costs.

Free devalues from the product in the minds of the customer. Customers quite reasonably wonder why it's free. Does the product have weaknesses? What is the start-up not revealing? Free is often associated with low quality. You can't come up with a compelling reason for the customer to pay for the product so a start-up gives it away, hoping the customer will find the must-have virtue. Another hope is the start-up will get customer feedback about the product. Free may mask product flaws. How much can one expect from something that's free—after all, you get what you pay for? And if customers give feedback, do you really want to incorporate features into the product that are needed by users who will never pay?

Free *does* work when the paying customer is not the person receiving the direct benefits from the free service or product. Websites and newspapers are examples of this approach. The customers are the advertisers who pay to promote awareness of their products among the readers, who are consuming the content and information for free. Free calendar programs work because the user organizes their lives and the provider can sell market research data to companies about the users — you can tell an awful lot about people from knowing their calendar entries. Free gets potential customers to try something that they wouldn't otherwise on a sample or trial basis.

What can you expect from Freemium models? I've seen many start-ups present the results. About 90% to 95% of customers opt for the simple, free version of the product and 5% to 10% of customers pay for the premium, full- featured version. An example of a Freemium model is PDF document technology. The Adobe PDF readers can be downloaded for free, while Adobe charges for the PDF creator. There are lesser known companies that provide a simplified PDF creation tool for free and charge for the full featured version. The question becomes: can you find enough power users who are paying customers to make the business sustainable?

Many bootstrapped start-ups cannot sell to customers in Silicon Valley. There are a lot of venture-backed start-ups in Silicon Valley. The expectation of customers is that if you are a start-up then the product should initially be free. However, this is not possible for bootstrapped companies because they don't have venture capitalists paying their operating expenses. Bootstrapped companies need revenue today. Therefore, many bootstrapped Silicon Valley start-ups don't sell into Silicon Valley; they sell only outside the valley because outsiders are more willing to pay.

Establishing the initial price is part of the customer discovery process that takes place during product development. To remove pricing as a consideration, ask the customer if they would use the product if it were free. If the answer is no, then you haven't discovered the right set of product features. If the answer is yes, then you've at least defined a desired product. Now, ask the customer if they would pay some outrageous price for the product. By mentioning an extreme price, you are hoping the customer will respond emotionally and tell you that you are crazy, the product isn't worth more than a particular sum. Aha! You now have a guide for pricing. Customers have a habit of asking for the world and in the back of their minds is the price they are willing to spend. Many customers imagine that requested additional features will not add cost for them. Pricing isn't so much about how much a customer is willing to pay as much as how much the customer is willing to pay to solve their problem; in the case of some consumer products, it's a matter of how much the customer is willing to pay to get what they want.

This short case study illustrates some of the considerations of pricing. This networking start-up developed specialized software for the Gigabit Ethernet market as an emerging technology. Back then, worldwide there were only 50 companies that could use the software. Today, the market is larger because the emerging technology is mainstream. The start-up's intent was to validate the market and generate revenue to cover operating expenses and invest in further development. This company was bootstrapped and not externally funded. With their initial release, they sold six licenses for $650,000 each. As the emerging technology was hyped, more of the potential 50 customers called to obtain licenses, but most complained about the price and were not willing to pay the licensing fee. When asked about an acceptable price, they almost always mentioned a range of $50,000 to $75,000. Consider the start-up's perspective; with their $650,000 pricing they were able to generate $3.9 million in revenue and it required only field support for a handful of customers. If the start-up had sold the product for a lower license fee and captured 100% of the market, they would have generated *less* revenue and would have needed to employ far more people to provide field support, thus incurring a much greater operating expense.

Pricing can be a roadblock. At one point Internet service providers were charging $24.95 as a monthly access fee. When one provider tried to raise the price to just $29.95, customers turned to other providers. The barrier was $25 per month. Today, as many nations consider the Internet for vital economic well-being, they are devising national broadband plans to create accessibility for all their citizens. In the evaluation of the proposals, the prices citizens will be asked to pay has gone beyond the typical deal-breaking level.

Pricing must take cash flow into consideration. How a large established player can price a product or service may not be how a start-up can price, given limited resources. A large company providing a service that requires equipment at the customers' premises and an on-going monthly service fee will often place the equipment on location at no charge and require a long-term service contract that guarantees them a monthly fee. While a start-up providing free equipment may create a nonviable financial burden, the start-up should consider charging the customer for the equipment and foregoing the monthly service for an initial set of customers. Getting the cash into the start-up for the equipment may be a great financial relief and if the service is a success, the loss of a monthly fee for those initial customers may be a wash in the long-term. Start-ups based on a capital intensive business model need to find a CFO early in their corporate life.

Likewise, start-ups may be able to follow a non-traditional industry pricing to the customer's benefit. The pricing model can be an initial differentiator, but it will not be sustainable as the competitors will eventually adopt the model too. The software business once was dominated by perpetual licensing schemes by which companies collected a large upfront licensing fee for the software and charged an annual maintenance fee and low cost upgrade fees. While the bulk of the money was collected upfront, this scheme made it difficult for the development budgets for follow-on releases. The term licensing scheme arrived whereby software licensing was sold for a three year term with annual maintenance fees. At the end of the term, the customer had to repurchase the software license at the full price. The customers enjoyed a lower upfront fee;

under the perpetual scheme it took customers years to realize savings from the resulting gains in productivity.

Venture-backed start-ups also have problems with pricing. Some start-ups incorrectly price their product below break-even, hoping volumes will materialize and eventually economies of scale will allow them to reach break-even. But when the anticipated volumes don't appear as projected and the funding runs out, the company can collapse. While there were some customers that wanted or needed the product, there weren't enough of them.

Service pricing is often a plethora of schemes and often depends on uniqueness of the task, volumes and customer expectations. When hiring a service, there are two common customer perspectives. The first is when an expert is hired and in this case, the customer usually has no intimate knowledge of the skill, e.g. hiring a surgeon. The second is when contractors are hired temporarily to accommodate a spike in workload. If you are hiring professional subject matter expert consultants, standard pricing is a multiple of the hourly wage for an in house, full-time employee — particularly if the client does not have a crisp definition of the work. Furthermore, hourly rates can give the perception of a cost effective solution. The client may think it will take one person 30 days to create a software module, but it will take several people a year to create what they want. Fees for customized software can be millions of dollars, but most customers are concerned primarily with results and development always seems easier than it is. Most service providers know if they told the client the expected total they might not put out an outside contract. In cases where the task and its development are well defined, price is commonly fixed. Auto maintenance and repair is an a la carte business model; routine services are fixed fee whereas repair services are hourly fee services. A la carte fees let the customer choose. Creating options for the customer—fixed fee, hourly fee, a la carte or pay as you go—gives the start-up time to consolidate their pricing scheme.

Customers always have reluctance to price. It always costs more than they expect or hope. When someone starts looking for a house to purchase, they almost always have a list of features they want and a price range in mind. As the home buyer starts looking, they quickly realize that to get the desired features they will have to spend more than anticipated; on the other hand, to maintain the price the homebuyer must eliminate some desired features. Most customers can afford to pay the price for the product even if they don't want to pay the greater than anticipated price. There is a difference between a customer's willingness to pay the price versus the real ability to pay. The questions then become is the customer desperate enough for a solution to pay the price or can the start-up justify the value of the product to the customer? Consumers buy more on emotion than benefit analysis; in the case of home buyers, everyone needs a place to live, but few need a 5,000 square foot house..

With corporate customers, price reluctance may be the result of procedure instead of value. Purchasing in corporations can be process-oriented and the price of a product can create a headache. Once I had to break a software license into modules so no single invoice exceeded $25,000; therefore, no manager would need approval from several levels of upper level management. Start-ups have the advantage of being flexible in their invoicing.

There are a lot of philosophies regarding the question: "To bundle or not to bundle?" Because of cost and complexity, point solutions almost always win. A product that tries to solve everyone's problems will find itself with a gazillion features aimed at solving *everyone's* problems. Most users use only 10% of the features; however, each user tends to use a different 10%. The problem is that every user must pay for all the features. Users also like to keep features simple. No one likes to take a long time to learn. Consider the trend in de-bundling: sell the base product and allow the user to customize the base with plug-ins, widgets, and add-ons. Look at Wordpress blogging software; it is a base and then other software pieces are added to make a customized rich user experience. Once we all purchased music albums. We wanted only few songs on the album, but we had to buy an album featuring a dozen of songs at a high price. Now we all buy single MP3 versions of songs. Conversely, consider Microsoft Office software, in which more and more applications were bundled and sold at one price. Car manufacturers sell option packages for the base car; you can't pick and choose individual options, just combinations. Sales people often don't like to sell bundled products. They must have expertise on more than one product. A sales person now has to tell a customer not only how one component of the bundle benefits the customer and why it is better than the competitor's version, but also how a 2nd, 3rd or 4th component in the bundle does the like. Customers simply want to solve their problems in the most cost effective fashion. The real question becomes: can the start-up provide this to the customer and become a profitable company?

Will increased volumes lower the offering price? Not necessarily. When portable DVD players were introduced, prices were well over $500 for a player. Today, prices are under $100. The devices have not become any more sophisticated; the features of those sold yesterday are the same as those sold today. Volumes have gone up considerably, as just about everyone has a portable DVD player today. This does not always happen. In the early days of the car industry, the car manufacturers chose to add new options instead of lowering prices, thereby maintaining pricing through continual features augmentation as volumes increased.

This story is about a healthcare and wellness start-up offering products and services directly to the consumer. They initially tried to offer a la carte product and services centered on their technology, and customers paid on a per service basis. While they were able to attract initial customers, customers stopped follow-on services after a few months. The start-up was bleeding red and only investor funding was keeping them from shutting down. The next approach was to abandon the pay per service pricing strategy and offer only a non-refundable annual service fee. Customers still didn't return for follow-on services after a few months, but they had paid for an annual service so more revenue flowed into the company. Fewer people purchased the annual service, but the higher average selling price (ASP) compensated for the lack of volume. This stopped the hemorrhaging, but the company was still in the red. They believed the annual service fee was the way to go—but how to improve upon it? The next step was to increase the average selling price and increase volumes. To increase volume, they brought in a finance company to provide a monthly payment options and more than 80% of customers chose the payment plans. Volumes increased dramatically. This moved the company closer to break-even. The next step was recognizing that consumers felt better about paying for an annual service contract if they walked out with a bag of tangible items, so they introduced a required starter set that was an additional 50% boost in the ASP. Even though this was a massive price increase, volumes increased because the financing program made the price jump acceptable. Nonetheless, the company wasn't at break-even. The next boost added an option to pre-pay for additional services and products. This finally brought the company close to break-even just as the funding had run out. Eureka! Then came the great recession and the pricing strategy built on good times. The product and service offered were a nice-to-have and expensive proposition, not a must-have. Customers were spending thousands on these products and services, nicely wrapped up in non-refundable annual fees. Volumes dwindled. Advertising couldn't be increased as it had been a crushing burden from day one.

The solution was to return to step one and try a new pricing scheme to accommodate the recession. This time, the investors would not provide further funding. Short-term service fees were introduced and the annual ones were still offered as the deep discount versions. Volumes continued to dwindle. The majority of operations were shut down, wiping out all expansion over the previous few years. The underlying technology upon which the services were based, which offered the market differentiation, was replaced by another company's technology — in hopes that the new technology would bring customers. The new technology slashed margins dramatically and volumes continued to fall. Product sales were eliminated to go to a pure services business model. A second and yet third type of financing programs were introduced—no improvements. Volumes continued to dwindle and advertising no longer generated sufficient leads. In the end, the company perished. The blame was cast to sales' inability to close the deals; in turn, sales blamed the pricing. Pricing is often a convenient scapegoat, but rarely the true reason. So what went wrong? A pricing strategy based upon value was never established. It was let's try something and see what happens. If it doesn't work, keep changing. The start-up calculated what they needed to charge to break-even with what management considered an achievable sales process. The start-up needed an 80 percent sales process, which meant 80 percent of leads needed to become qualified leads, 80 percent of qualified leads had to agree to a sales call, 80 percent had to buy the basic package, and 80 percent had to purchase add-ons. In addition, the price had to be one of highest in the marketplace. The approach was to let price create the perception of the quality of the offerings because the customers could not easily judge the real quality before use. Profits were to come from the unused pre-paid products and services that were never delivered. It wasn't pricing based upon value, but pricing based upon operating expenses. The start-up never realized who the customer was—or why their customer was buying at all. The actual customers did not match the target customer profile. The technology that was their key differentiator did not hold great value for the customer and wasn't the reason customers bought the service and products. The moral of the story is pricing is never as easy as it first seems.

The Team

The Right Team, The Right Stuff at the Right Time

None of us is as smart as all of us.
-Ken Blanchard

When investors evaluate a start-up proposal, they report that about 25% of the final decision is based on the team. Many of today's hi-tech products are so complex that no one person can understand every aspect of the product or how to bring the product to market. Despite the complexity of the products, it still is less important than the team. Why? Because it is easier to correct problems with the product than to fix the team. The success or failure of a start-up hinges upon the team assembled. The right combination of people at the right time is indispensible. A start-up team can be more than the founders and the employees; it is also the corporate advisory board members, mentors, customer advisory board, and even the investors.

The Founders and the Start-up Team

At the beginning, there is nothing but an idea. Investors are funding a team and a belief that they can do what they say they can do. Not only does everyone need to perform a diverse range of functions, they all need to work in concert.

People hire people like themselves. If the founding team isn't good, it is not likely to get better. Three roles are the most important to fill: the chief technologist who will lead the product's development; the chief marketing person who will lead the effort to understand the customer, promote awareness for the product, and figure out how to make money with the product; and the visionary who can inspire and influence the skeptics among the customers, market, and investors. The visionary must be able to "wow" people. In the early stages, the marketing person may be the same person as the visionary, but this eventually diverges as the workload increases.

Experience is of the utmost importance when there is only one person to perform a job function in a start-up. Never confuse the number of years someone has worked with years of experience. A candidate may have worked for 15 years, but they might not be able perform at a level beyond someone with only a few years of experience. Credibility is based upon accomplishments, not years worked. Whoever is on the team will be scrutinized by investors, and sometimes also partners and customers. Investors always ask: who is the team, why they are on the team, what role each will play, what have they worked on in the past, and most importantly, what have they accomplished in previous positions? Because of the small size of a start-up, employees participate in many aspects of the business.

Management and leadership are also crucial. Just because someone has years of experience performing a specific skill does not mean they can lead a team. Nor does giving someone a managerial title make the team follow that person's direction. Start-ups thrive with experienced staff members. Seasoned employees will not follow someone's lead without believing in the task and the project's direction, and respecting the opinion of the leaders. Start-ups must attract and build small, highly effective, performance oriented teams.

An important question for entrepreneurs to answer is: would you hire yourself? Most first time entrepreneurs want to be the CEO. It seems glamorous.. But if you don't want to raise money, you shouldn't be the CEO. In early stage start-ups, CEOs spend most of their time raising capital. If you don't want to manage people, you shouldn't be CEO. If you don't want to be held accountable for everything that goes on with the company, you shouldn't be CEO. The best definitions I've read are the CEO is the glue that binds the organization together, and the CEO is the blank white page of a book that holds and pulls the words together in an order that makes sense. It's a tough job—if you aren't committed to it, you won't do it well.

Advisory Boards and Mentor Capital

Advisory boards can fill in the gaps with the direct team. Mostly, they advise the company on management or technology issues. Many investors believe an advisory board should be less than six people. These are usually term board members, as who is needed to advise a start-up today is not necessarily those needed in the future. For an advisory board to be effective, the start-up needs to keep in regular contact with the board members. This contact can be through email updates and monthly lunches to discuss company progress. It doesn't have to be a formal board meeting. These advisors will implicitly act as references for the start-up with potential investors because investors will contact them for information and analysis.

Mentors are people you can go to for advice or who will act as sounding boards, but they don't want a formal relationship.

Start-ups can have informational meetings with venture capitalists to get feedback about their proposals without asking for funding. Likewise, start-ups can have meetings with executives of companies to discuss their business proposal. Many times, there are similarities between businesses in different industries, and a start-up may want to transfer a methodology from a seemingly unrelated business. A mentor may not want to commit a lot of time to the start-up, but might be willing to advise on a casual basis. Another form of mentor is a stake advisor; these mentors place a small amount of funds in the company in exchange they promise to advise the company whenever asked.

Customer Advisory Boards

Customer advisory boards bring the end user into the team. This advisory method has been used to great success; for example, Mexico's *Grupo Reforma* newspaper uses citizen editors and community boards in the "ultra-local" concept. This approach allows newspapers to be embedded in communities. The newspaper has created 12-14 editorial boards, corresponding to every section of the newspaper. The community board terms last for one year, and these boards guide the issues and stories covered by the sections.

Investors

Investors look at a start-up objectively. They aren't emotionally attached to the company or the product concept. When seeking investment, don't be shy about asking the potential investor how they can help your start-up reach its full potential. Some investors talk with their start-ups on a weekly basis. Some network among the investment and industry communities, keeping an eye open for others that can further the ambitions of their portfolio companies. Whether or not investors decide to be active or inactive participants, they too can be a great source of mentor capital and connections. I have been involved with start-ups that have struggled to raise follow-on rounds. And I have been involved in start-ups where the CEO was not raising the hundreds of millions in funding; instead, the investors were raising the funding.

Myths and Common Mistakes

A START-UP OF ONE. The slogan "Army of One" doesn't work for investors. A team is not one person. The CEO can't be the Chief Everything Officer. Investors are willing to help you build a start-up team, but not the entire team. Investors don't want to invest in one person shows. If the founder can't convince others to join in the company, why should the investor believe the founder can convince customers to buy the product? A start-up needs to demonstrate the diversity of roles needed to make a company successful and appreciation for all necessary skills.

RIGHT PEOPLE AT THE WRONG TIME. Hiring a great experienced person at the wrong time is a misstep. You shouldn't hire an experienced senior executive from a large, established company for a seed stage start-up. Often, the executive's best skills are making incremental process improvements, driving efficiency into an organization, and expanding an established market presence. When confronted with trying to build a team, a product, and market presence from nothing, they are often like fish out of water.

Several scenarios are plausible. These executives may take the position because they want someone to pay them while they are looking for their next big move in another large company. Other times, it's a matter of the grass looking greener in the other pasture. How many executives left their Fortune 500 company positions and jumped into start-ups after seeing fellow executives become rich quickly and easily in the technology boom? Lastly, these people are used to empire building; they are judged by how many people report to them and I've seen start-ups in which this becomes a goal. Most executives are career-minded and aware of how title, responsibilities and accomplishments appear on their resumes. When they resign and move on, the start-up takes a big hit. However, there comes a time in a start-up when hiring these executives becomes advantageous.

THE LOPSIDED TEAM. A highly successful individual is lopsided, focusing on developing and honing a specific set of skills. The same does not hold true for organizations. A recipe for failure is that the founders build a lopsided team, heavily weighted to one specific function and neglect other functions. Often, this mistake occurs because founders stick with what they know best and trivialize other necessary functions. Some technical founders believe, "If you build it, they will come." Unfortunately, they often learn the hard way that products don't sell themselves. Sales founders believe, "If engineering can build it, we can sell it." Sales people can be eternally optimistic: "If only the product were ready now, I could have closed a multi-million dollar deal today." Then when the product is complete, the deals don't materialize. Marketing founders believe, "It is technically impossible not to develop the product." In other words, they believe product development is a short and easy task. The founder and CEO of one start-up had a sales background and while the software product was at least two years from general availability, business development and sales people in the organization outnumbered engineering developers by 5 to 1.

SKILLS ARE NOT EVERYTHING. While a seasoned person is a great asset, it's not everything. Start-ups need people with a can-do attitude, a strong work ethic, ambition, and the ability to reason. Don't be impressed by a lengthy list of specific tools and technical skills. If a software person can think and program in one language, they can easily pick up and program in a different language. Someone who doesn't think well cannot efficiently program in any language. If a sales person is a closer, they may wait until someone else presents them with the deals to finalize and close. A closer may not be willing to be the sales or business development person who also searches for the deals. Start-ups cannot afford to compartmentalize job functions. Secondary traits matter as does broad experience.

A TEAM IS NOT A COLLECTION. A team is not a random group of individuals simply willing to work on the project. This may seem obvious, but it is amazing how many times a group of disparate people form a start-up with no clue about their organization roles or skill sets. Every team member serves a purpose and should have expertise and a focused job function. Often, this means a team member performs a needed job function—not necessarily what he wants to do.

THE LOW COST EMPLOYEE. If you have only a lone attorney, human resources, finance, or marketing person, they *must* know what to do and how to do it without help. When there is only one inexperienced person in a job function, numerous mistakes and lost time are inevitable. Even though the employee is inexpensive, it's better to hire a part-time or interim person through an outside firm.

BOARD MEMBERS FOR FUTURE POTENTIAL. While some advisors may also be investors, it is not recommended that an advisor be placed on the board because of a potential future investment, particularly if the advisor represents a venture capital firm. If the venture capitalist doesn't take a stake in the next funding round, then other investors may shy away because the obvious question will be: Why didn't this board member invest?

OVER EXTENDED BOARD MEMBERS. One consideration is whether or not prospective board members have enough time for your project. If a potential advisor is already guiding 12 or more companies, he/she probably doesn't have the time to truly contribute.

In the early stage of the start-up, the credibility of the team matters most. If an entrepreneur only has a pie-in-the-sky idea, investors have little evidence by which to judge the team other than past experience and accomplishments. The more customers and market traction the product has, the less of a factor is the credibility of the team. It's hard to argue with tangible results.

An exceptionally strong team with a mediocre product will get a better reception than a weak team with a great product. Remember, it's easier to improve a product than it is to make the people behind it better.

A hi-tech start-up team is an entrepreneur team embarking upon a high risk adventure. To be successful at all, regardless of whether it's the next multi-billion dollar company or just a few million, means you've won against extraordinary odds. The team is one of the top reasons for success. Choose it wisely.

Considerations for Finding the Team

And I'd say one of the great lessons I've learned over the past couple of decades, from a management perspective, is that really when you come down to it, it really is all about people and all about leadership.

—Steve Case

Attracting and hiring a staff from ground zero is tough. The first step is to know who you need to hire, when you need them, and why you need this particular person. The last criterion is the most challenging. Most founders know their job functions well, but they often don't understand the importance of the other functions. Just ask an engineer what a marketing person does and vice versa. Now imagine the founder is that engineer, and they need to hire the marketing person, the Chief Financial Officer, and possibly a range of only vaguely familiar job functions.

The hiring person should write a list of how this new person will specifically contribute to the organization in the short term. Long-term goals can be more general. For every job function, there is someone who freelances at it. Find these freelancers or contract firms, invite them to come and talk with you, and ask them how they could contribute. From there you can fashion a job description. The quality and diversity of the team is crucial to the success of the start-up, and if the founder is an engineer hiring a marketing person, it is easy to hire the wrong one.

Finding the people with the right skill sets when they are needed is difficult. A company rarely hires their ideal candidate. After a while, it seems as though the person you want to hire is an elusive mythical creature. The work needs to done and start-ups don't have the luxury of waiting. Most people hire the best available candidate at the given time, not their ideal employee.

Some start-ups hire only people they worked with directly in the past and as the organization grows, they only hire based upon referrals from current employees. This approach works, but only take recommendations from your best employees. The old adage is true: "Birds of the feather flock together". I once had an engineer in my organization and the rest of the technical staff complained about the quality of this person's work. However, they interviewed and hired another engineer recommended by this person. Eventually, we had to let both people go, which was disruptive in a small start-up and management had to calm the other employees who didn't understand why these people were let go. Similarly, having pleasant conversations with someone in the break room doesn't mean that person can perform their job function well. Another approach I've seen is to hire anyone willing to work for them and hope you get a few really good people to carry the average. I've seen start-ups be successful with it because they had a lot of funding or needed rapid growth.

So what about hiring experience versus inexperienced staff? I have seen development groups that are 90% college hires as well as groups of 100% experienced hires with 10 or more years of experience. I once conducted a study at a corporation to evaluate the mix of experience and college hires for a software and hardware development. Many companies seek college graduates or junior engineers because they cost less than experienced employees. Not surprisingly, the study showed college hires are the most ineffective members of the technical staff. The analysis gave them an average productivity index of 300. Staff members with 5 years experience reached an average productivity level of 750. Those staff with 10 years experience produced an average of 2200. After 10 years of experience, productivity gains were marginal. Experience does matter a great deal in productivity. Salaries for staff members with 10 years experience are typically twice that of a college hire. This gives experienced hires a much better price to performance ratio than the more inexperienced members. However, even in today's tough job market, people with 5-10 years experience are in demand and are difficult to attract to a start-up company.

As a start-up, it's not easy to attract employees. The founders believe in the vision and are passionate about the project, but potential employees are skeptical and the more experienced candidates have the biggest concerns. When the economy was better, potential candidates were willing to work for start-ups because they could quickly find another position if the start-up collapsed. Currently, great candidates are less willing to get involved in a start-up because if it fails, finding another position could be difficult. Second, if the candidate took a pay cut to join the start-up, the salary reduction may continue into the next position.

Serial start-up people enjoy creating a product and company. They know what it takes to get one up and running. They love the work environment and the challenge. A start-up needs to search for experienced hires that have not only the technical skill but have worked in start-ups before and thrive on the start-up environment.

Due to financial or recruiting challenges, start-ups often turn to volunteers, interns or a part-time work force. While the idea might seem great in the beginning, these team members can be frustrating to manage and slow to produce. Volunteers want something in return for their participation, usually more than just stock options. Maybe it's the opportunity to work with a particular technology or to expand their professional experience. Whatever it is, the start-up needs to fulfill these objectives or the employees will quickly leave or be marginally productive. Volunteers often commit only a few hours per week. Because volunteers are not around for 20 or 40 hours every week, it's often difficult to discover what truly drove them to volunteer. Volunteers work well with short-term tasks, i.e. editing articles versus programming a software module, which could take months to complete. Recently I sat through an investor presentation, where the start-up was able to develop Internet software exclusively with volunteers. One investor asked why it took two years to develop the first release of the software; in his opinion it should have taken at most nine months. The answer: everything moves more slowly with volunteers.

College interns are great. They are enthusiastic and eager to work long hours, as they have few other responsibilities. They usually have the financial backing of their parents and aren't overly concerned about compensation (if there is any). They are more interested in the experience and exposure to the organization as it will serve them upon graduation. However, they are usually available only for short periods of time, and are truly dedicated only when school is on break. I once time hired a full-time doctoral candidate and the work was in her field of study. The employee wasn't concerned about how much she earned because her primary motivation was gaining experience. However, her school work always took precedence over the company, and she often called in sick, didn't show up, or left early whenever work was due at school. When I worked for IBM, a particular R&D manager claimed at the fall progress meeting every year that he had fallen behind schedule because his departed flock of interns left him in a lurch. The keys to success with interns are is to realize how unproductive they are and to assign appropriate tasks, as well as succession planning.

Good part-time employees are difficult to find. They are more dedicated than volunteers because they are paid and feel obligated to be productive. The best part-timers I've ever dealt with were the attorneys who negotiated one of my start-up contracts, licensing agreements, and partnerships. These attorneys were fabulous — they were highly skilled, responsive, focused on being productive, and efficient. I dreaded whenever our work was moved to a full time partner; the service declined as my start-up didn't get much attention. On the other hand, I hired a part-time engineer on the recommendation of one of my better engineers. This part-timer had a day job and wanted to moonlight. He would spend extra hours at his full-time day job, then he wanted to play on a soccer team or act in a local community theater, then he wanted to spend time with his family—and only then was he willing to work. He would turn in time cards with only a few hours a week recorded, much less than the required 20 hours per week. Not only did we have to let the person go, but we had to recover from the lack of productivity. If the part-timer has another full time job, then pay for deliverables, not by the hour (regardless of whether payment is cash or equity). Part-timers work well when they are seasoned and don't have another full time job. If the company's regular employees come into an office, require these team members to do so too. If they don't want to work in the office, consider paying on a deliverable basis.

Part-time employees or volunteers are used in marketing as well. Marketing requires the person to be out among the customers and industry gatherings, and this is difficult to do on part-time or volunteer basis. It's difficult to track people down, set up appointments, and attend meetings on limited hours. Appointments that could normally take place in a week stretch to four or six weeks. Only the rare individual has the discipline to work from home effectively or to perform the volunteer role in additional to their normal day job. The best odds of succeeding with this type of work force are in roles where the job function requires little collaboration and the tasks can be broken up into small segments. Even then, it's best to have an office where they are scheduled to come to work at specified times. Like it or not, workers without paychecks aren't committed. While the approach works with unpaid interns, these interns are supported by their parents. An intern is looking to gain experience. While it still won't make the situation as good as full time, paid employees, it's the next best alternative.

As much as most people don't want to admit to the uncomfortable truth, we all engage in what I call unconscious discrimination. People hire people like themselves. If a company was founded by an immigrant, the majority of the staff will have the same ethnicity. If a company is founded by Ivy League school graduates, many of the staff are Ivy League graduates. If the founders all have PhD degrees, many of the staff will also have PhD's. This is usually more obvious from an outsider's perspective than from the inside. I once interviewed a Russian immigrant for a start-up whose employees were 85% Asian Indian and one of his concerns was his lack of potential opportunity in the organization. Another start-up I was involved with was founded by researchers and tended to hire people with research backgrounds. Consequently, the staff liked to hold meetings to discuss what was theoretically possible, but little tangible work was ever accomplished.

I have had the pleasure of working with many excellent teams in start-up companies and I have seen the not so good ones as well. There is no single right team. The fate of a start-up often hinges upon the quality of the team assembled, and having the right combination of people at the right time is the key to success. While founders may not understand someone else's job function, having an appreciation for it can go a long way. Not only does everyone need to perform a diverse range of functions, they all need to work in concert to achieve the end.

Convincing People to Join the Team

Never doubt that a small group of thoughtful,
committed people can change the world. Indeed, it
is the only thing that ever has.

-Margaret Mead

You have finally found that person that you want to join your start-up. They're interested as well. So how do you get them join? In the beginning, there is no human resource person to handle hiring; the founders will need to negotiate compensation with the workers.

Experienced hires, who have worked for large corporations, are used to the compensation packages offered by these companies. Candidates may place a price tag on each of the benefits of their current job and expect to be compensated for the loss of those benefits. For example, if a candidate is currently covered by a 401K plan with matching company contributions, the candidate may expect to receive the matching portion in salary. They may calculate the value of after work educational benefits, and even though they don't use them today, they will ask for the additional salary to cover the loss of the benefit. Candidates from large corporations can also ask for salary boosts due to the risk associated with a start-up. Such candidates do not thrive in a start-up environment. Typically, they expect a 9-to-5 job that is safe and secure. The itemized comparison between their former corporation and the start-up will not stop at the job offer. They will also point out the lack of resources and equipment available at the start-up. For example, they will complain about the number of servers and software licenses available per person.

As goes the current economic conditions, so goes a start-up's ability to attract people. As the economy heats up, it becomes more difficult to hire interns, college hires and experience — and the more attractive the opportunity has to be. Today, many start-ups have large number on non-paid employees, often unemployed and looking to keep their skills sharp while searching for a job. These volunteers offer little consistency since they often go away when a paying opportunity emerges.

When I first started hiring people, I was given advice that still holds true — if you can't offer a candidate a compensation package within 5% of their expectations, you won't get the candidate.

Sales is a pay-for-performance position and sales people are evaluated based upon performance. While sales is one component of the start-up team, the sales staff members tend to be truly view themselves as individual contributors. Sales people expect marketing to determine the applicable market segments for the product, promote the product in these markets, and to generate the leads. A sales team is an execution team. The sales team often works on a salary plus commission basis. It's not unusual for them to ask for a minimum guaranteed level of commissions when a start-up is new and unknown. Good sales people don't want to work on a salary only basis — the more experienced and confident they are of their sales skills, the less salary and the more commissions they want. Therefore, attracting great sales people at the inception of a company is difficult; they often adopt a wait-and-see attitude. An early stage sales person wants to see the volume and traffic generated by marketing that isn't captured in revenue because the company can't close sales. Sales people won't stay with a company unless the commissions materialize. One way to filter sales people is to see how assertive they will be. If you have their resume or contact information, send them an email and ask them to call you to set up an appointment for a meeting or a phone call. Most sales candidates don't call, and by that response alone, they have filtered themselves out of consideration.

Marketing is a difficult position to fill. Customers want to know how your product is different. Investors want to know how you will differentiate the product and the company in the eyes of the customer. However, marketing as taught in schools distills marketing to a step-by-step recipe. Corporations have created procedures and guidelines for marketing. Therefore, while marketing is supposed to focus on defining and creating that which is different, it often ends up as a blur of commonality. Start-ups should think about how well that marketing candidate is promoting themselves in the job market, or how process versus creative-oriented. Today, social media marketers are common. Every start-up wants to use social media marketing. Everyone knows what it is and how it should work, and there are plenty of success stories, but few understand how to use social media marketing from ground zero.

Sometimes what makes the difference is not monetary. It's amazing what people will do for a job title. You may be able to find free labor, but these people are still getting something out of the work. I hired a Director of IT who wanted the title of Director of IT and Networking. If a few added words are what it takes to make the candidate happy, then agree. It's amazing the number of times I've seen start-ups lose good candidates over something that simple.

It's far easier to convince a college-hire to join a start-up than an experienced hire. In the start-ups I've been involved in, college-hire and interns accepted about 80% of the offers and experienced hires about 25% to 30%. Why the gap? Experienced hires think in terms of their next job. They are hedging their bets. If the start-up doesn't work out, and historical data suggest this outcome, then how can they get a boost into their next career move? More than likely, an experienced candidate is at least partially supporting their families and is accountable to their spouses — their children aren't going to give up music lessons so Mom or Dad can work at an interesting start-up. Candidates who are not only experienced but also serial start-up people know that you need to negotiate everything before joining. Start-up employees are often asked to take a pay cut and most know annual raises are unlikely for years. Serial start-up people know that whatever position you are hired into is likely to be your position for the next few years, and if there is growth, the start-up will hire from the outside rather than promote from within.

In 2005, an age discrimination law suit was filed against Google, which revealed the average of a Google employee was under 30 and only 2% of the employees were over 40. This is typical of a young high technology company, which in early years is heavily development oriented. Much of the programming and engineering work is rudimentary, mundane, and task oriented. It's career appropriate for college hires. Experienced hires want a much bigger role in defining and creating the product, guiding the team, formulating the direction of the company, and interacting with the other functional areas. A seed to early stage start-up will often begin with a core of less than 20 experienced people, and once it expands, more college hires and junior level staffers arrive. An experienced hire needs to have a career appropriate role in the organization.

How to Keep the Team

Coming together is a beginning. Keeping together is progress. Working together is success.
-Henry Ford

Contrary to the expected, the number one reason people leave a company is not monetary; it's because they feel unappreciated. Start-ups are so focused on meeting milestones that management sometimes neglects simple acts of praise.

A common mistake I see is the founder's or CEO's inability to empower the employees to do their jobs. Most start-ups are small. Start-ups thrive because of the experienced people in the company. If a CEO or founder treats everyone as mere assistants and must approve of everything done in the organization, disaster is looming. Experienced employees don't like to be micromanaged. It happens a lot in start-ups. Particularly today since funding is limited, start-ups are less than 20 people, and start-ups may have people working for free or only for equity. A company can't grow and achieve greatness this way.

Fear does not motivate employees; it pushes them to look for new jobs. Start-ups are not lavishly funded and it's likely that the next round of funding will come just in the nick of time. Don't let employees worry about having a paycheck next month.

A popular method of retaining people is known as the golden shackles, offering the employee more options on an extended vesting schedule. While everyone has a price, it is not necessarily monetary. I've seen many people resign despite the stock options left behind.

Initially, start-ups hire from outside the company because there are few people within. Unfortunately, this practice often continues. As the company grows, a start-up company's inclination is to continue hiring from the outside. When they do promote from within, it's usually a last resort because they could not find a suitable candidate in the job market. This is the point where the early team members leave the company — the financial gain is dwindling and they are unable to grow as the company grows.

Anyone who has ever been involved in selecting and hiring candidates will eventually hire someone they regret hiring at a later time. Bad hiring choices cannot be always avoided. A small percentage always passes through the filtering process. The real question is what the management team will do about it. More often than not, most managers prefer not to confront the situation, but let it continue. I have rarely seen anyone fired in a start-up. Letting people go is stressful for both the employee and the manager. Performance issues are more difficult because they are subjective, like beauty is in the eye of the beholder. Other members of the staff do not necessarily see the performance problems. The problematic employee is viewed by coworkers as the personable guy they chit chat with in the break room. Firing one employee will alarm everyone. They start to wonder how management perceives them and whether they are the next to go. It may take weeks to calm the organization and return to business as usual.

In my experience, the initial start-up team has about 18 months of exuberance for the product and the start-up company. The next wave of new employees has at most 12 months of enthusiasm before their new jobs become routine. If members of the current staff develop a negative outlook, new staff members will lose their enthusiasm even quicker. As a result, people will not be as productive as they should be. Management must address the negativism before it spreads.

As the company grows, so changes the personality of the new employees added to the staff. The initial team is a completely different breed from those joining the company with a hundred or even thousands of employees. As a company matures, it becomes more reserved, more bureaucratic, more process oriented, and attracts more 9-to-5 employees — and more traditional means of retaining people become more effective.

Product Development

Why Is the Schedule
So Elusive?

*The only time I really become discouraged is when I think of
all the things I would like to do and the little time I have in
which to do them.*

— Thomas Edison

Why are product development schedules so elusive, like
trying to hit a moving target? I have never been involved in nor
have I ever heard of a project going according to plan. This is
crucial in a start-up because sales can't sell what R&D doesn't
have available, and investors don't fund hype and vaporware
for very long. A staff almost always creates a schedule starting
from the present and works forward in time. The completion
date is whenever everything gets done and the schedule rarely
considers disruptive events. Management almost always starts
in the future with the desired completion date and works backwards to schedule the program, identify resources, and define
contingency plans to mitigate risks that occur along the way.
Management thinks in generalities and company-wide impli-
cations, and the staff thinks in specifics of their own job functions. In a nutshell, the R&D staff tends to be ultra conservative, whereas management tends to be overly aggressive, and
somewhere in the middle is the true schedule. Instead of com-
promising, both try to convince the other that they are right.
How to get the two to act as one?

A process I have followed is to present the project to the
staff and first let the technical staff define its schedule from the

bottom up. I have often instructed my managers not to voice opinions prior to the staff establishing their schedules. I want the staff's honest input. I don't want them trying to please their managers by telling them what they think the managers want to hear. Once a clear idea is established as to what the technical staff thinks is doable, then refining the schedule with a top down approach is possible.

A bottom up approach is more difficult than it appears. I've found technical staffs love to complain about the schedule. It's a favorite corporate past time. Management and *their* schedule become the convenient scapegoat whenever the project doesn't go as expected. However, when given the opportunity to define their schedules, the staff complains just as much. The most common complaint is they don't know every intimate detail of the proposed project and therefore don't want to be held accountable for schedule inaccuracies. It is as though they want to define a forward looking schedule on hindsight instead of experience. I have found staffs to be 25% to 33% overly optimistic. On a conceptual level, the project always seems less complicated than it is; ultimately, the devil is in the details. Likewise, they never account for the little things that go wrong like network problems, resource sharing issues, power outages, software licensing problems, personnel turnovers, materials delivery delays, and so on. Whereas, management tends to trivialize the design complexity of the product features and overemphasize business considerations.

I have further emphasized this bottom up approach by using the staff's schedules to determine individual milestones for performance reviews and bonuses, as well as making the staff managers dependent on how well his/her direct reports meet their individual milestones. I prefer quarterly bonus plans because people will work harder to be rewarded in the short term.

Most schedules are created at the inception of a project—and projects often take years to complete. The future is uncertain and the market changes. This is especially problematic with high tech start-ups where the original product concept can be a very distant relative of the one that goes to market. So while there is usually tension between R&D and management over the development schedule, marketing gets added to the mix and further compromises are required. Product definition happens in parallel with development and inevitably results in changes to the original specification. This sends the product schedule into revision and technical people dislike chaos being thrust into their efficient and beautiful designs.

If everyone is to truly "buy-into" the schedule then they must be included in its creation and know their input is valued. False buy-ins are no good. I worked with a manager whose group reported being 99% complete for more than a year, only to have him leave and subsequently discover the group was less than 50% complete with their portion of the project.

Ultimately, what matters is reaching the goal within the desired time frame. The schedule is merely a tool. This is really a matter of getting people to perform their seemingly disparate, individual tasks and to listen to others in the organization. The goal is not the completion of the product development phase, but the success of the product in the market place. Everyone needs to be flexible. Schedules can be aggressive, realistic, and attainable, but *must* involve the participants in the changes.

Development Schedule Gone Astray

There is no shortage of ideas just the will to implement. Time is becoming the most crucial strategic weapon and the pressure is on to compress time as much as humanly possible.

— Adesh Jain

Is your project behind schedule? Is your staff ignoring the development schedules? Are you constantly issuing revisions, never pulling in but always pushing out your schedules? Admit it; we've all been there. Once you are so far behind schedule, do you start to eliminate product features or reduce the number of target applications? Product development schedules are important. They set clear expectations and clear deadlines. They are critical in a start-up where future funding may be tied to performance against the schedule. Even in established corporations, funding may hinge upon meeting schedule milestones. This first segment will illustrate how NOT to approach a staff with a schedule.

Software Schedule or Miracle

One day at a Silicon Valley start-up, the development staff was called to a project meeting where the management team presented the development schedule. The schedule was defined by the management team with no contribution from the technical staff. The management team stated that they had worked backwards from a delivery date proposed by an important potential customer. First, the hardware schedule was defined and then the software effort was shoehorned into the schedule. In this case, the software and hardware efforts were equally intensive and complex. Unfortunately, the software schedule became a one day effort and it was scheduled to commence and complete on the 31st day of September. Many of the sharp engineers and programmers quickly smirked because as they all knew that September only has 30 days! You might think this was an oversight, but no. The management stated that with enough preparation and efficiency, one day was enough. As the presentation wore on, the staff had the expected eye rolls and mutterings. As the staff exited the meeting, I heard such words as "ridiculous" and "absurd". When I asked the staff why they didn't speak up, they said it would be useless because the management team didn't want to listen so the "project would progress at its own pace", and that is exactly what happened. The software effort took more than a year.

Exercise in Futility

Soon after the inception of another start-up, I saw a management team derive the most detailed scheduled I have ever seen. They scheduled tasks for a four year program across all functional areas—down to the hour. The company had only a handful of people yet managed to determine what hundreds of potential new employees would be doing hourly for the next several years. The schedule was difficult to read and continued ad nauseam page after page. Although the schedule was often touted by the management team as the "plan of record", the employees never took it seriously and the program proceeded at its own pace. However, the Board of Directors *did* take it seriously and was not happy when the company did not meet the plan.

End Goal

What happened? If the staff has no schedule to work towards then progress is haphazard. It reminds me of a fish on the shore, furiously flapping as it desperately tries to reach the water. The flapping creates little forward progress and expends tremendous energy. Unrealistic schedules have the same effect as no schedule at all. They are dismissed as unattainable or ridiculous. Add the potential of creating a communication barrier between management and staff, and you are in real trouble; you may never know the true status of the project at any given moment.

Some Marketing
Implementation Issues

Advertising Lessons

Many a small thing has been made
large by the right of advertising.
— Mark Twain

When I started my first company, I knew nothing about advertising. Now I know more about it than I thought I'd ever know and realize that I have been manipulated for years.

The start-ups that have taught me about advertising have been e-commerce ventures, traditional brick and mortar stores, business-to-business companies, and professional associations. I learned many lessons the hard way through ineffective campaigns I managed and from interaction with experts guiding my campaigns. One crucial lesson: what works well for a big and established business doesn't necessarily work well for a small business or start-up.

The purpose of mass media advertising is to reach the masses. If you're incurring the cost of reaching the masses, you should be getting mass responses. From the beginning, be clear about the goals and determine how success or failure will be measured. Tracking results is imperative. Recording when a customer responds to an ad isn't enough; *who* responds is as important as the *number* of responses. Each ad is aimed at a particular audience. You need to validate the assumptions of whom, when, and where. Did you have the expected number of responses and are they increasing? Unless you challenge the assumptions and ask these questions, how can you know the difference between a campaign that needs more time to be effective and one that is simply a failed strategy? Advertising is a numbers game: make the numbers work to your advantage.

Effective advertising can be achieved only through experimentation. Advertising always seems too expensive and too slow at getting results, but there's no alternative. It's not just the cost of the media buys but also the cost of experimenting with the various channels, determining which one works best, and learning to optimize the performance of each channel. The selection of a publication is important, but so are where you place the ad, the size, the color scheme, the wording, and the competitors for the audience's attention. You could place your ad in the right journal yet get little or no response. On the other hand, the perfect ad may not resonate with the audience because it's in the wrong publication. Bring up the topic of pay-per-click at any meeting about advertising, and you'll hear immediate groans. Everyone, particularly start-ups, has spent large sums trying to find the best keywords. Also, bidding costs can be prohibitively high. A well-known email marketing company has an annual expense of $4 million to maintain its first page ranking for organic search results, and spends another $4 million on inorganic search with its pay-per-click exceeding $25. A common misconception is that the Internet and social media are free, but when labor cost and time are considered, these new approaches are as expensive as in any traditional media. All media present their challenges.

Lessons Learned

1. Trust but verify. Often advertisers try to sell you ad space based upon the size of their audience, the geographic area of distribution, the frequency of publication, and so forth.

Such information tells you nothing about their effectiveness as a channel. A good approach is to find previously published advertising material and check with the companies that advertised (even if the publication provides references). If you're considering an ad in a tradeshow program guide, obtain last year's guide and call the companies that advertised to learn what their results were. Media salespeople always want to sell long-term contracts. Even if the discount is great, avoid such contracts until you know the channel works.

2. To gauge the appropriateness of any media, check out their current advertisers. Have you ever noticed that ads on highway billboards and public bus panels are always the major players? How many local businesses advertise on a highway billboard? How many are instead Ford, Toyota, IBM, Microsoft, and Apple? There is a reason: these channels are cost prohibitive to small companies.

Note when competitors or similar industries are running their promotions. They have a lot of experience advertising to the same audience and know best when to reach the targeted customer. Car dealers know to advertise late in a week because most people buy cars on weekends. Weight loss programs don't advertise late in a week because no one wants to start a diet on Friday. Watch your email box. When do you receive notices about online store offers, newsletters, or tradeshows?

A medical clinic and day spa service business advertised in the local newspapers and through email marketing. The clinic tried both approaches for a year or more before the ads disappeared from both media. Look back at previous advertisers and see what they did; it's an indication of how well the media worked.

3. If readers get something free, it's not as effective for advertising as a publication with paid readers. All trade and

newspapers boast about how many readers they have, but many give away their publications. The readers don't necessarily look at or read such publications. My local town newspaper boasts a large circulation because it is mailed without charge it to all businesses and everyone's houses. Likewise, many online information sites have free email newsletters, but the recipients don't necessarily read the newsletters. Similarly, organizations report that a percentage of their membership rolls have particular demographics, but it doesn't follow that those members paid for those memberships. Some organizations offer free memberships to certain individuals just to be able to use them to promote the group for advertising rates. Advertising rates reflect the audience size. The more people, the higher the rates. Media buyer beware!

4. Large companies tend to advertise in the largest reaching media, such as *The Wall Street Journal* or *Time* magazine, but not in local or regional publications. It's easier for them to deal with national media organizations than a gaggle of small, niche, or local media companies. By contrast, targeted and niche marketing work best for start-ups, which have a limited budget. It's better to dominate a subset of customers in a niche market or a locality within the niche than have merely a slight presence everywhere.

When the target audience has numerous choices, pinpointing the most promising choice is difficult. It's harder to be effective in TV than in radio. In television, viewers are loyal to a program, not to a network. Most viewers have hundreds of channels and flip between them looking for an interesting show. With radio, listeners usually have their favorite three stations and change between these few.

The concepts of frequency and reach apply equally to newspapers, television, radio, or the Internet. It's more effective to dominate a time slot or customer segment. Instead of advertising in twenty-five magazines, advertise in a few and give the appearance of being a national brand to that customer segment.

5. Advertising strategy must be consistent with pricing. The average selling price of one start-up's product was $1,200, but the advertising cost to obtain a single lead was over $300. Competitors were spending less than $156 to obtain an actual customer. By contrast, if the product price is $25,000 and the advertising cost to obtain a sale is $300, then the producer may have a viable marketing strategy. A viable strategy lies in the advertising cost per lead and advertising cost to obtain a sale, not in the size of the advertising budget. When choosing a promotion approach, consider if it can be sustained long enough to prove the assumptions; if it fails, there is enough budget left to try a different approach.

6. Advertising is about trade-offs. There is no right answer; many approaches can achieve the same results. It is, however, a zero sum game. Location is a good example. A location, either storefront or tradeshow floor position, can give a start-up more visibility with passer-by traffic. With more visibility, less can be spent on paid advertising to get customers to the location. Likewise, there can be trade-offs between advertising versus labor and travel costs associated with direct marketing and sales.

7. On a whim, I found a useful (and free!) Silicon Valley marketing group through Meetup. The peer group organization invites professors from the local business schools, local advertising and marketing experts, and SMB companies to share their experiences. The practical and specific advice and discussions on strategies make the group invaluable.

8. An agency or a media buyer will be expensive and most won't handle small companies. Despite the costs, it's still less

expensive than the DIY method because they can "ramp up" faster than you can without them. Agencies have many clients and are paid on commissions for the media buys. They are not going to get you better pricing, but they can get better positioning for your ads, help you change the original contract if the ads don't work, and potentially find personalities that will provide editorials, reviews or endorsements. Advertising is an art. Even an agency will need to experiment with promoting your product and company, and this is a time consuming, costly trial and error process.

When dealing with an agency, start-ups must be very proactive. They need to track the results diligently and feed them back to the agency. What worked well five years ago may not work well today, and what worked for a similar product might not work for yours.

9. Potential customers will check out your company's website before contacting your company. As the expression goes, "If you're not findable of the Internet, you don't exist." Human behaviors are predictable; most will check out your website within a few days of the promotion. If the ad is effective, you should see a spike in traffic or a rush of phone inquiries. Thirty days after the promotion, the response will have died out. Many Internet searchers steer clear of a website's info@company. com email address. We've all had numerous experiences of getting no response from the info@ — it's like publishing an 800 number and not answering the phone. Initially, you may place a specific person's email, which will encourage viewers to send email inquiries more than the @info address.

The cost of advertising is simply inevitable. The hard truth is products don't sell themselves.

How Much Will Marketing Really Cost?

He who seeks for gain, must be at some expense.
— Titus Maccius Plautus

For most startups, the risk of failure is with the marketing and widespread customer acceptance, and setting realistic expectations for budget is crucial.

A general business rule states most markets consolidate to 3 to 5 big players. What will it take to effectively market a new gizmo in an existing market? First consider the competitors in the market today. How much market share does each one have? Studies have shown there are only a few cases to consider. If one or two companies have 75% or more of the market share or if one company has more than 40% of the market share, it will be difficult for a startup to compete against these dominant players. In either case, marketing expenses typically need to be 3 times that of the dominant players in order to break into the market. If the market share is otherwise, the market is fragmented and marketing expenses will need to be 1.7 times that of the existing competitors. Startups have the easiest time penetrating a market where all competitors have 25% or less market share.

Does this mean if the dominant player spends $10 million on marketing that a startup also needs to spend this much? Of course not, but it can be used to determine a benchmark for the startup. The start-up can target regional areas or a segment of the target customers. It does allow the start-up to determine such numbers as the marketing cost per lead and the marketing cost per sale. If it works out to be $350 per lead, does that mean if you spend $350 you'll get a customer. No, because there is a minimum you need to spend just to reach a large enough pool of customers to be able to calculate statistics. However, it does set realistic expectations and maximum bounds for the startup. If a startup has a marketing budget of $300,000 and the established players have a $300 cost per lead that says a dominant player would expect 1000 leads. With a 1.7 to 3 times dilution factor, a startup should expect 333 to 589 leads for the same budget. One approach is to work backwards from the goal. If a startup wants some number of customers at the end of the first year, what size of budget do they need to have to do so?

Amazon.com is a very successful e-commerce website that began in 1994. There are plenty of such stores available on the Internet today. If an entrepreneur were to start an Amazon competitor today, how successful would it be? Blogging has the same characteristics. Many of the blogs with large followings and traffic are those that were started when blogging was young. The blogoshere is very crowded today and experts say that the techniques used to popularize those early blogs won't work as well today. Investors like proven markets - young markets that are growing, but not ones that are mature and saturated. It's not to say one can't make money in a mature market, it just requires more capital to overcome the incumbents. The entrepreneur has a different perspective than the investor. The investor has the ability to select a company from among many proposals in different markets. The entrepreneur is building a company based upon his expertise and can't chose from among many different markets. An expert in Internet security software shouldn't start a pharmaceutical company. For most start-ups, this means being highly focused and targeted as to where the marketing budget is directed and having realistic expectations of the size marketing budget. For a small company, the difference between spending 1.7 or 3 times the competitor's budget is huge. The marketing can't explode such that it stifles or sinks the company.

Testimonials and Editorials as Promotion

A good basic selling idea, involvement and relevancy, of course, are as important as ever, but in the advertising of today, unless you make yourself noticed and believed, you ain't got nothing.

— Leo Burnett

Many advertising and public relations consultants claim that getting editorials written about your product will produce a better response rate than advertising. Some business managers even say editorials and consumer reviews build a business, and advertising maintains the business. How effective is editorial content? And is it *really* free?

Consumers trust editorials and other consumers' opinions and reviews, but consumers mistrust advertising. It's a learned response based upon experience. Kids believe in commercials and packaging. My daughter believed that if she ate a Gushers fruit snack, her head would temporarily explode into the fruit that flavored the snack. Somewhere between childhood and adulthood, we learn advertising and sales people don't tell the truth and they will say anything to get a prospect to buy. While not always true, we've all experienced it enough to be skeptical of advertising.

Editorial content takes different forms. Companies can get journalists to write stories about the product, bloggers to review the product, radio personalities to try the product and talk about it on the air, celebrities to endorse the product, and customers to provide testimonials. Companies such as Yelp and Amazon get customers to review products and aggregate the opinion of the crowd for a rating, the closest thing you can get to a trusted, word of mouth referral.

Recently, I managed the advertising, marketing, and sales effort for a consumer start-up. The company used radio, television, newspaper, outdoor advertising, business co-marketing, and Internet advertising. Consumers' perceptions and responses to advertising—whether it appears in traditional media or the new digital form—is no different. The expression, "The more the world changes, the more it stays the same" holds true.

For radio, our strategy was to gain endorsements from local radio personalities. They would use the products and provide their opinions on the air. Hiring a local advertising agency was critical if personalities were to at least *try* the product and consider endorsing it. Dealing with the personalities is a lot harder than it sounds. Some were a pleasure to know and work with, others were divas. First, you need to build a lot of time in the schedule to work with personalities. The agency needed to find willing personalities. Some personalities were interested immediately; others had to be weaned for 6 months. The company wanted to interview and educate each personality about the products and services, and likewise, the personality wanted to interview the company and meet everyone they'd be working with. Finally, we had to be worked into the personality's schedule. During all the set-up activity, the company needed to advertise and general commercials were broadcast in the interim. Personality endorsed commercials produced four times the leads as the general commercials on the same stations.

Find the best subject matter experts in academia, universities or national laboratories and have these people endorse the product or service. This goes a long way to building credibility in the eyes of the investors.

Consumers mistrust advertising because it is paid for by the companies selling the product, but there is a common misconception. While radio personalities were not paid, they weren't actually free. The agency had to be contracted to engage the personalities. The start-up had to agree to a minimum amount of advertising on the stations and this affects how much the radio station pays the personalities. The start-up had to provide both our products and services to the personality for free, and since the company also offered a service, we had to pay the labor of the employee to work with the personality. Even the crowd opinion is not necessarily free. When Yelp enters a local market, they must build up a large database of reviews quickly for users to see their service as valuable; therefore, Yelp initially pays reviewers in new markets. The opinions given by the consumers may be honest, but they are still paid for in some way.

Understanding Sales

What Sales Is and What It Is Not

Every one lives by selling something.
— Robert Louis Stevenson

Most people, who have never done sales or been trained in sales, simply assume a sales person meets with a customer and talks about the start-up's product or service—with no more to the process than that. This is a common misconception.

Everyone must know how to sell, regardless of their job function. If you are presenting to investors, you are engaging in sales. If you are presenting technology at a technical conference, you are performing as a sales person — building credibility for your start-up, the product, and the development team. If you are having a technical discussion with a potential customer, you are in a sales process. If you are interviewing a job candidate, you are selling the company. Everyone sells in many ways. It must not be a thoughtless process.

Since most early stage start-ups are mostly technical people, it's amazing the number of founders I've encountered who tell me they have no one for marketing or sales. Nonetheless, they tell me they have no time to do it, they don't like doing it, and they feel no need for any training, even for a short workshop. The common excuse: their budgets do not allow them to hire anyone or would be better used for something else. Therefore, it ends up being done badly, neglected or not at all.

I was working with a software start-up and the founder was very technical. On the third meeting, the CEO showed me the business plan and asked for my analysis. My immediate reaction was that it read like a PhD dissertation; it focused on the technology and actually incorporated pages of mathematics with detailed algorithms. The CEO mentioned the various company advisors and proudly told me that he wanted only advisors that truly understood the nuances of the technology. As the conversation continued, the CEO admitted that he was weak in sales and marketing. He was performing these roles because he didn't want to hire someone for these job functions unless they also had a PhD in computer science. When I asked if he had taken any short-term workshops to develop sales and marketing skills, he said no—it was too costly. The company was just about out of money, they desperately needed a cash infusion in a month, and he wanted to focus on the technology. If someone doesn't like a role, they may agree to perform but do so grudgingly, thereby putting the company at risk.

Social networking has popularized the notion of "going viral". Many founders say they want to use a viral approach for building sales. They *really* mean that they want to remove the marketing and sales expense as a line item from the budget. It's the new way of saying, "If we build it, they will come." They plan on abdicating the sales and marketing to social networking. While there are those rare proof points attributing their success to going viral, it's the equivalent of betting your income on winning the lottery. Sales isn't this easy!

Sales is not a PowerPoint presentation, which allows everyone to create presentations effortlessly, and thoughtlessly. A start-up must excite the listeners: they must *wow* them. When was the last time you were wowed by a PowerPoint presentation? Most likely never. It's not long after a PowerPoint presentation begins, we usually wonder: *When will this end?* I expect the dry and mundane, and I am not often disappointed.

Speakers often use the bullets and numerous words as a crutch—a compensation for poor speaking skills. Since so few people use PowerPoint effectively, most people merely imitate bad presentations; they assume that a PowerPoint presentation is required. It's the difference between a good actor who can make the character come to life and the bad actor who woodenly recites from the script.

Demonstrations and mock-ups allow the audience to quickly grasp the product concept. But everything has its time and place. Like weak PowerPoint presentations, demos are often used poorly. They can be too long, too detailed, boring and just like every other company's demo

At Comdex one year, one of the big software vendors had a grand new release. Instead of giving a dry product presentation, they hired a local theater group and script writers to produce a short stage show about the upgraded features. Ten years later, I still remember the product and its new features. Contrastingly, I remember nothing about the hundreds of other presentations I saw that week at Comdex, most of which used PowerPoint slides. Stories make products more memorable, as does visualization.

One of the best board demonstrations I've seen was for a networking device. Mostly they are black pizza-like boxes with many blinking lights, indicating data flowing through the box. You can't get much more boring. This start-up wrote front-end graphical software to show the data moving rather like a train station; one could click the icons and see individual packets being transferred, or one could move up and see pictures moving across the network and being reconstructed at the destination. The board members were impressed. The start-up had only one person to quickly cobble together this software, but it had a deep impact on the viewers. It was spectacular because it stood in contrast to the dull, pizza box demos.

Sales is not effortless. It is a structured, orchestrated process. Sales systematically researches potential customers, seeks them out, tries to understand the customers concerns, presents the product as a solution to the customer's problem in a manner that is palatable to the decision makers, and negotiates a purchase, Good sales people do not just wing it. Sales will spend time investigating a prospect, particularly if the potential customer is a visible company. That is, they are publicly traded and information about the company is readily available, or they have gained traction with press coverage. With such companies, it's easy to research their product lines are, how they are each doing, what the financial performance has been over the past few years, and so on. Prospects want to do business with companies that understand them. Therefore,

Understanding the Sales Process

Internalize the Golden Rule of sales that says,
'All things being equal, people will do business
with, and refer business to, those people they
know, like and trust.'

—Bob Burg

There is often little or no distinction between sales and marketing in a start-up. Marketing is like the architect that designs your house; he speaks with the homeowner, taking vague ideas and developing concrete blueprints and plans. Sales is like the general contractor who builds the house; he executes the plans.

What did I just do? I made the reader visualize the concept. It makes the idea stand out from the mundane noise of the boring facts, words, and features. Stories and analogies make people remember, as do humor and demos. But too much of a good thing produce the opposite effect and bring the audience back to the noise.

Marketing does the prep work; sales is the next step. While both interact with the customers, marketing does so to define the product, search for applicable markets, build awareness, and generate leads for sales. Marketing does not try to get the customer to buy the product, negotiate the deal, and get the customer to pay. That's the sales team's role, and it's not easy.

The first step for sales is finding the customers. It's time consuming to search for the right customer. Sales often seems like looking for needles in a haystack. The Internet, the sales portal to the largest group of prospects, attracts small percentages of customers. There are nearly seven billion people in the world and about 25% are Internet users. Therefore, about 1.7 billion prospects can be reached online. Yet, we are wowed by the website that attracts one million, three million, twenty-four million users —less than 1.5%. And if the start-up is using a Freemium business model, then the number of paying customers is a small percentage of the less than 1.5%.

Once the sales person has found a customer then they must get to know the customer. Customers want to do business with organizations that know them and understand their problems. The sales person must define the issues and deliver solutions. It sounds straightforward. But how many of us want to discuss our problems with other people, and the nitty-gritty details as well? How long must you talk with a person before they feel comfortable enough to air dirty laundry? The answer is 20 minutes. Studies show it takes about that much time before a conversation becomes divulging and interesting.

Not all customers are the same; some are analytical, some are relationship oriented, some are emotional. Whether it's a consumer or business-to-business product, the person making the purchasing decision responds differently to different approaches. A good sales person can tune presentations to the customer's style. This performance must be dynamic and improvised. In fact, many sales people have formal educations inl psychology.

Revenue growth requires that the sales process be repeatable and scalable. This can't be done without regular practice. A sales person can't become effective unless they make enough sales calls every week — no more than a person can become proficient at any skill that's rarely practiced. Sales growth must hinge upon the average sales person, not the one-in-a-million sales person. If a company has many sales people, but only 1 or 2 bring in more than 80% of the revenue, then the start-up has a problem. The sales process will become "tuned" to the style of those stellar performers. Likewise, a start-up has a problem if 80% or more of the revenue comes for only a couple of customers.

When a consumer calls a service for information, the person answering the phone must be trained in what to say, how to say it, and when to say it. When a sales person meets with a prospect, the sales person has been trained what to say, how to say it, what to present, and what non-verbal clues to give. When a sales person leaves a voice mail message for a potential customer, the message itself has been carefully constructed. The sale person is controlling the interaction with the prospect; the process is well planned. This process does not stay the same; it changes. As a start-up broadens its customer base, the different types of necessary customers are incorporated into this process. The first sales people in a start-up must define and develop this process, so more sales people can be trained and sales becomes a predictable process.

The Sales Call

People get caught up in wonderful, eye-catching pitches, but they don't do enough to close the deal. It's no good if you don't make the sale. Even if your foot is in the door or you bring someone into a conference room, you don't win the deal unless you actually get them to sign on the dotted line.

— Donald Trump

Preparation goes a long way with a fruitful sales call. Research as much as possible on the companies and people you will be speaking with before the meeting. Before even going into a sales call, think about the impression you hope to make. What do you want them to remember a week from now? What is the objective, what do you want the people to do, what information do you want to obtain? Be specific. Here is an example of a sales call for the Easy Weight Loss Company.

Step 1. Greeting

In this phase, the sales person establishes a rapport and an atmosphere for the meeting.

Step 2. The Discovery Process

The discovery phase allows the sales person to determine the customer's problem or need, what the customer wants, and the customer's dominant buying motive.

Customers buy on emotion. Even those who appear to weigh all the facts will use those facts to support the decision they have already made emotionally.

The questions to ask while reviewing the client questionnaire are:

- **Why do you want** to lose weight **now**? Why do you feel Easy Weight Loss Company can help?
- **What did you like most** about other diets or diet programs?

(Never ask what they disliked, as it devalues their previous buying decision. If there was a large issue with a competitor's product, they will take the opportunity to mention it without prompting.)

- **What improvements would you like** in the other diets or programs?
- **What is your ideal** diet or diet program? **Why?** (This is the top of the customer's pyramid and establishes the dominant buying motive)
- **What do you do best** when on a diet or when you are trying to lose weight?
- **What is your greatest challenge** when on a diet or when you are trying to lose weight?

The discovery process is the majority of the sales process. It should be a conversation. Careful about how many notes you take during the initial meeting. Some customers view note taking during a conversation as a form of interrogation, and other customers see it as a sign of genuine interest in their problems and concerns.

Step 3. The Presentation Phase

The presentation stage is the selling phase. A sales person shouldn't start selling the customer on their services and products until they know what the customer wants and needs. If the sales person does the discovery properly, the presentation gives the customer meaningful information. Products should be presented in the following sentence structure: *claim* because *feature,* which means to you *benefit* and the real benefit to you: the *dominant buying motive*.

Presentation Sentence	Interim Word used to Bind Segments
CLAIM: generic good news	because
FEATURE: fact that has proof	which means to you
BENEFIT: advantage of the fact and/or why is it a good deal	and the real benefit to you
DOMINANT BUYING MOTIVE: connect to emotional benefit	

An example of a presentation sentence would be, "We take the guesswork out of dieting **because** we test, measure, and profile you with latest medical equipment, **which means** you'll lose weight more effectively and **the real benefit to you** is you'll fit into that bikini sooner for your summer vacation."

Psychologically, customers come up with a negative when presented with a fact, which is why a benefit should always follow the statement of a fact.

Step 4. Trial Close

The trial close is asking the customer if your product will meet their wants and needs. It can be phrased by starting with "in your opinion."

In your opinion, do you feel you could use a program like ours?

The question has only three possible answers: yes, yes but, and no. If you get *yes*, then close. If you get *yes but* then go back and keep selling. If you get *no* then handle the objection.

Step 5. Handling Objections

Handling of objections should be phrased as follows.

- Obviously you have a reason. Do you mind if I ask what it is?
- Just suppose that _____ was not an issue. Do you feel you could then _____
- I understand _____
- Other customers have had similar issues and we solved this by _____

In the first segment of the response, the sales person asks the customer to define the problem. In the second segment, the sales person is verifying the problem — it's best to give the customer's words back to them. *Do not* paraphrase, as you may interpret their words incorrectly. The customer cannot argue with their own facts. In the third segment, the sales person shows empathy for the customer — always use the word *and*, never use the word *but*. When you use the word *but*, the listener remembers only the latter part of the sentence; however, they remember both parts when the word *and* is used. In the last segment, the sales person is establishing credibility with the customer by explaining they have seen similar issues (always use the word *issues*, never the word *problems*. Problems are for the competition). Finally, the sales person presents the solution.

Step 6. Close

The close should be short and sweet. It indicates to the customer that the sales process is over. Ask the customer for the final decision. It's never a matter of *how* to close, but rather *when* to close.

Look for the buyer's signal: that is, anything the buyer says or does to indicate a mental buy or mental rejection. Examples of positive buying signals are that the customer asks how to pay for the service, or indicates the service looks like it would work, or asks about guarantees or rebates. An example of a mental rejection is that the customer stops paying attention. In the latter, the sales person must regain the customer's attention before proceeding with the initial consultation.

Other Hints

Don't leave it up to the customer to call back. Always ask how much time they need before you can call them back, and establish a specific day/time.

Don't thank the customer for coming until the end of the initial meting

In value-added selling, you are selling the reduction of cost and/or the avoidance of future cost to the mutual gain of both parties. That is, price is last in establishing a value-added service. Never give a price; establish value. Never give anything for free; instead, give a sample. In this example, the avoidance of future cost would be the avoidance of another weight loss plan in the future with our lengthy maintenance program, which establishes permanent weight loss.

Sales People

*Sales is a process, the process of building a relationship
and turning a skeptic into a believer and making a
stranger your friend.*

-Steve W. Martin

Sales people are odd balls in hi-tech start-ups. Product developers are the many and sales people are the few—perhaps even the one. The development team often misunderstands the sales people. Large companies implementing enterprise level social networking note that developers take to social networking like ducks to water, but sales groups do not. The difference is the developers work in a collaborative work environment—where the completion of a working product is everyone's goal; everyone's work is connected, and everyone must work together. A common complaint among developers is the development team member who does not share information with the team. Sales people are loners, and their performance plans are all about their individual performance — how many sales calls they make, how many deals they close, and their average sale price. They have to answer to the management team about every deal they are working on — going through its status and its potential. What will get sales people bickering is doling out of leads—how leads are distributed among the sales staff and how territory boundaries are defined.

Sales is one of the ultimate pay-for-performance positions. Good sales people know they will make more money from commissions and bonuses than from salary. Sales people have to be thick skinned because they hear "no" a lot from prospects.

They have to be aggressive and persistent just to talk to the prospect. They have to know people and how to manipulate them and the conversations. Sales people are psychiatrists for the customers —getting the customer to tell them everything about themselves so they can determine if the product can benefit them, how it can help the customers and what will make this customer buy. And like patients, customers do not readily divulge this information. Sales people get a high from closing the deal; it's the thrill of running a race and crossing the finish line first. Once the race is over, it's over. Sales people do not often want to deal with the customer afterwards. The pleasant, understanding, and responsive sales person during the sale process becomes the deaf ear. Therefore, customer service is a separate organization from sales!

Sales is often the first to be blamed for a product's failure. As such, a good sales person will not join a start-up unless they believe they can sell the product in suitable volumes. Sales are also the first people to desert a company. If anyone knows whether a product is viable or not, it's the people introducing the product to the customers. Sales has specific revenue goals, so they know exactly what's needed to keep the start-up financially afloat. Sales leaving a start-up is a sure sign of trouble.

There are more not-so-good sales people than good ones. Sales is heavily commission based, so most employers are willing to let everyone try sales. It costs the employer little or no money to do so.

Not all sales people are created equal and they are not interchangeable. Some are better with consumers, while others are better with businesses. The sales cycle with a consumer is much shorter than the sales cycle with a business. Consumer-oriented sales people have told me they like to see quick results and they like to see how quickly they can persuade people to do what they want. Business-oriented sales people are relationship builders, working towards a big payoff over the long-term. Sales with consumers are more about emotion; sales with business are more about return on investment and empirical benefits. Even between consumers and businesses sales people, price anchors further segment them. A consumer-oriented sales person, who's good at selling $1,000 to $3,000 items, is not necessarily good at selling in the $100,000 to $500,000 range. Likewise, a business sales person selling a $3,000 product is not interchangeable with one that sells $1,000,000 products.

Sales people who can define and develop a repeatable sales process and those implementing the process are different people. A sales closer is a here and now person. They think in short-term, tactical strategies to get the customer to sign on the dotted line. A good closer may or may not be someone who wants to define a sales process and grow a sales organization.

Technical people tend to be introverted, analytical, and detail-oriented. Sales people aren't. This is one place where the tendency to hire people like yourself can cause difficulty in an organization founded by and staffed by mostly technologists. A CEO with an extensive sales background told me that if you put a technologist and a sales person together, they will dislike each other. It's an instantaneous reaction. If you are one of these people interviewing the other in a start-up, disliking the interviewee might be a positive sign.

In a start-up, where everyone's contribution is crucial, hiring the right sales people can be the difference between success and failure.

Funding

The Odds of Getting Funded

*This I do know beyond any reasonable doubt.
Regardless of what you are doing, if you pump
long enough, hard enough and enthusiastically
enough, sooner or later the effort will bring forth
the reward.*

—Zig Ziglar

What are the chances of getting funding for a start-up? It is estimated that at any given moment there are 6,000 new product concepts looking for funding in the Silicon Valley. There were about 2,500 start-ups funded by the venture capitalists in 2009 and only around 10% were new start-ups funded at conception; the bulk of the money flowed into companies already operating.

I am sure that every start-up is telling potential investors that they will become a publicly traded company. To go IPO is the ultimate goal of most start-ups. Why? Because where there is profit, there is progress and where there is the belief in the potential for profit, there is funding. There are 15,000 publicly traded companies in the U.S. and in the past ten years, venture capitalists funded around 30,000 companies. Only one-tenth of one percent of companies reach $250 million in annual sales. To put this into the investors' perspective, of the 2500 start-ups funded each year, only 2 or 3 of those companies will get to $250 million in revenue.

Venture capitalists track their contacts with potential start-ups much like any other sales process. Last year, one firm recorded 150 qualified leads from referrals or previously successful entrepreneurs. While VCs receive proposals from strangers, most report they rarely fund these projects. What happens to those 150 start-up proposals? They are reduced to 50 that receive serious consideration, and then 10 are selected to be pursued. Finally, only 1 is funded.

Likewise, most angel groups report receiving 600 plans last year, two-thirds from strangers. Of these proposals, 72 are considered, 36 are invited to present to an angel group, and 4 to 6 are funded: less than 1%. A typical investment was $300,000, and took a 25% to 30% equity stake. These groups look for start-ups that anticipate a total investment of $3 million.

How do you determine if a fund is right for your company? As a rule of thumb, the expected return of each portfolio company is the total size of fund. So if a venture capital firm closes a new fund of $200 million, that's what they want any one portfolio company in that fund to return back to the fund. Most funds invest in the first 4 years; the remaining years are for harvesting the investments. The fund's lifecycle is very important. If an entrepreneur wants to find out if a firm is tire kicking or really intends to invest, ask when they raised their last fund. Fortunately, any firm having recently raised a new fund will issue a press release about the new fund, and these are the funds the entrepreneurs want because they have the money to invest—and they have to invest somewhere.

The VC community has an affinity for providing seed funding to entrepreneurs that have brought them great profits in the past or who have been referred by those that have brought them home-runs.

All investors perform a due diligence process, essentially a background check on the entire proposal. The more accountable the investors are to others, the more rigorous the process. Venture capitalists and other institutional investors have the most meticulous procedure; they must answer to their investors and partners. They also have more access to any industry's experts and influencers. Groups of private investors try to perform a careful examination of the proposal, but not as thorough as the institutions. The lone private investor does less, and family and friends do the least. I have been involved with start-ups where the CEOs intentionally approached lone private investors for this very reason and have raised millions of dollars. Most first time entrepreneurs start with the venture capitalists because they've heard about them, it's easy to find out who they are, and they are the obvious place to start. More often than not, they will get no response.

A company creating a new market might be unprofitable for 5 or more years, while one in an existing market might be generating cash in 12 to 18 months. Investors expected a start-up to be acquired in 4 to 6 years, and an IPO to take between 7 and 10 years.

What grabs investors' attention is a start-up that already has customers and revenue, or something never before seen. Recently, a start-up got seed funding from investors in the Midwest — and the start-up was not located in the Midwest. The start-up promised these Midwest towns that they'd open up a customer service office there, bring jobs to the local economy, and they did.

What many start-ups don't do after talking to investors is to request more information. Ask what the next steps are. Ask what they thought about the company and product. Ask how they can help. Ask the investors what milestones are needed to receive funding.

Investors often admit that the more they know about a particular market space, the less likely they are to invest. On the other hand, they also admit that they don't invest in products and industries that they don't understand. It would seem most everything is non-fundable. Ultimately, only return on investment matters to investors. For example, a lightning start-up received a lackluster reception from venture capitalists recently because they viewed the industry as slow moving and company valuations are typically 1 to 1.5 times revenue, which didn't make it an attractive opportunity. At the same time, a lot of investors are chasing clean and green technologies.

First, realize that obtaining funding can be a long process. It is essentially a sales process. It is a search. Second, how can you move forward without outside investment? Then consider your best alternative to outside investors. How can you succeed without them?

Never Neglect Funding and Its Trends

A vision without resources is a hallucination.
                                                    —Unknown

Without capital, it doesn't matter how good your plans are or how fabulous the product concept is because you'll never make it a reality. Start-ups may not succeed even with the capital, but they certainly can't succeed without it. Likewise, nothing can be accomplished without the people to create the start-up's vision. Too often, funding takes a back seat to development, which leads to disastrous results. So while both money and people are required, money needs are a priority. While this seems obvious, many start-ups run out of money because they started to search for their next round of funding much too late.

Funding does not happen overnight. No potential investors will be in love with your concept and business plan; all will point out flaws and pitfalls. This is an important point most entrepreneurs don't understand. There is no shortage of product ideas being presented to investors, in fact, there are too many and most are very similar. Therefore, to whittle down the choices investors look for reasons NOT to invest. There are many reasons that they don't invest — maybe the market segment doesn't have enough growth or maybe the start-up has consistently missed milestones. In the end, investors vote with their dollars. Below are some actual conversations between investors and entrepreneurs.

Conversation #1:

Q: Are there any other companies doing this?

A: Yes, another start-up.

Q: How far along is the other startup and who are their investors?

A: They are about a year ahead of us, but are having difficulty gaining traction with customers. Their investor is ABC Venture Capital, an icon of the venture capital industry.

Q: Do you think that the clout and reputation of ABC Venture Capital will scare investors away from your company?

Q: Are you always going to be playing catch up with them?

Conversation #2:

Q.   What is novel or special about your product?

A: The revenue model. It'll be free to the end user and we will monetize it with advertising.

Q: Advertising is never a differentiation.

Conversation #3:

Q: What is the barrier to entry?

A: It's a first-to-market scenario.

Q: Do you have another barrier? Be careful of using first mover advantage as strategy. It doesn't often work and it resonates badly with investors. We've seen start-ups unable to capitalize on being first in a market.

The first time would-be entrepreneur or the outsider often believes venture capitalists love risk. This is not true. They may not be as conservative as banks in lending to businesses, but they do not throw caution to the wind and invest in every new product concept. Too many would-be entrepreneurs concentrate their attention on the product concept, but there's a lot more to making a company successful than the idea or technology.

Each venture capital firm has its criteria for investing in a start-up. I used to work for a major corporation with the traditional spring and fall planning cycles; one dedicated to funding projects, the other dedicated to reviewing progress and determining the future of every project. Every year the criteria changed for funding or continuing a program. And like a major corporation, the venture capitalists constantly change their criteria for funding. It's difficult to get funded if you don't know what they are looking for in a company today.

Just as in capital markets, timing is everything. Yesterday's hot technology is not likely to be worthy of investment today. Suddenly a funding wave erupts and numerous start-ups are dedicated to a particular concept. Every venture capital firm needs to have its play in a hot technology. Most of these start-ups will quickly flare up and flame out. There were dozens of WebTV start-ups, but only a few had any success. Remember the dotcoms, telecoms, application service providers (ASP), set top boxes, digital music hardware and software, and so on? Just search on clean tech, green and solar start-ups and you'll find a plethora of them today. Sometimes a concept is revived because the original was ahead of its time. Social networking may seem be the latest craze with the likes of Facebook and LinkedIn, but the concept and first start-up was Six Degrees, funded in 1997. Cloud computing and SaaS are closely related to ASPs. Find a niche, innovative or unique product, but don't fight a trend.

To spot a technology trend, look at the membership of industry associations and attendance at the major conferences. You'll find exponential growth for 4 or 5 years, then the organizations and tradeshows decline rapidly and most disappear. Just because John got funding last year for a technology doesn't mean every Tom, Dick and Harry can be funded with a similar idea this year. As the funding gains momentum, the benchmark for funding is raised. By the time a technology is widely reported by the trade press, the bulk of the funding wave has passed. And like the project funding cycle within large corporations, projects are funded and then reassessed at the next funding cycle.

In my recent discussions with venture capitalists, most have spoken about risk reduction. Their plans have included *not* investing in seed rounds that they felt were more appropriate for angels or private investors, not investing in emerging technology standards that have no market today, and investing in companies that can show market validation in less than a year. I've been involved with many start-ups and only two came close to demonstrating market validation within 12 months. It is difficult for a hi-tech start-up to go from ground-zero to any customer revenue or early adoption so quickly. A company creating a new market might be unprofitable for 5 or more years, while one in an existing market might generate cash in 12 to 18 months.

Hi-tech products can spend several years in development alone. In speaking with the angels, they have also expressed an interest in reducing their risks. Their plans include investing only in companies where the capital will be used to expand existing operations or product lines. These angels feel the initial seed funding should come from an entrepreneur's network of family, friends, and fools (commonly as the FFF Network)—who, I suspect, are also unwilling to fund ideas due to the current global financial crisis.

I know a founder of a privately-held company that has been in business for 10 years and he tells the story of dreading the family Christmas party every year. He initially received funding from his family and every year they ask him when they are going to see their money back.

If a start-up is lucky enough to hook up with a leading venture capital firm then money may find its way to the start-up. I've been involved in start-ups funded by the likes of Kleiner Perkins, USVP and Sequoia, and it's the connections and capital supply chain of the venture capital firm, not the management team's efforts, that secures the funding. At one such start-up, the management team was told when and where to show up for an investors' meetings; they were told that as long as they presented themselves well, the money was theirs. Those start-ups not funded by these giants of venture capital have a lot more difficulty in obtaining funding rounds. Several CEO's I know have been completely exhausted by the constant need to find funding, and some start-ups have even decided to hire a person dedicated to this task. One creative start-up hired away a managing partner from a venture capital firm and as a result, the start-up obtained the necessary funding.

Many times companies rest on their laurels after earning a round of funding, thinking they have finally made it. However, start-ups close all the time due to lack of funding in subsequent rounds. Even those with revenue can be shut down due to their lack of potential for return on the investment. Once you get funded, the next step is to stay funded.

Best Alternative to Investor Funding

Bootstrapping a company is on most entrepreneurs' minds these days. Attend any meeting of angels or venture capital and you'll hear how entrepreneurs should focus on bootstrapping and not seek funding until they have a proven product concept. The translation is we don't want just an idea; show us your paying customers today. One venture capitalist recently said start ups not only need innovative products and marketing approaches, but that entrepreneurs must consider funding innovations. It's a great idea. Innovative financing sounds good, but how exactly do entrepreneurs do this—and what does it even mean? I have not heard any specifics on the matter, only vague notions. The basics of raising money for a company or project have not changed in hundreds of years. How did Christopher Columbus raise funds to sail to the new world? How did the Renaissance artists raise money to fund their projects? How did Larry Page and Sergei Brin raise money for Google? The old-fashion way: they convinced investors of the worthiness of their ideas. If you can't get outside funding, what are your options?

There are three common ways for bootstrapping a company. They're not innovative or clever, but they work. The first method is to find one or more companies with the problem and offer consulting services to develop a custom solution. Later, use this work as the basis for your product. Second, form a start-up with two groups: one offering contract services to solve related problems for customers and the second developing your product and funded by the contract services. The third:

be a reseller in the market and use the sales organization to fund the development of your own product in the same market.

In the first method, the start-up locates a business customer that needs the product and is willing to hire your company to develop the product. The trick is to maintain joint rights to the work. This will allow the start-up to modify and introduce a revision to the general market. Companies are willing if what is developed is not proprietary and does not represent a competitive advantage to the developer. Proprietary features will belong to the company but the rest of the development effect is usually acceptable for joint ownership. Why would most companies do this? In today's economy, companies don't want to increase headcount but still need the work done. Second, the proprietary aspects will be developed by the company itself as their competitive advantage in the marketplace and the company will want to keep this part of the development in house. They are willing to let an outside firm develop the industry standard pieces of the product, so they will let you modify and resell the rest. They will also consider the development of the more standard features to be less risky.

This method can be used for several iterations before the final product is reached. If the final product envisioned can sustain a viable business then many companies must be looking for a solution. The original company funds the first version of the product, and then a second set of companies further develops the first version under contract. The second sets of companies pay to license the first version and then pay contract services to further expand the product for their use. Joint rights to subsequent versions must also be established. Thus, the second version reaped the benefits of another round of quality assurance testing and input from additional marketing teams. Multiple customers will force the development team to conceptualize a general product applicable to many: one that is extensible, supportable, and maintainable. This approach can be continued until a product is ready for the general market.

The companies contracting with the start-up are funding the development and are testing the product, offsetting the development costs and funding the project without consuming equity. The latter benefit is the quality assurance (QA) process, helping the start-up create an error free product for general availability. This is important; QA can cost at least as much—sometimes more—than the creation of the project. The start-up will also benefit from a better understanding of the customer and this will extend into their marketing efforts later.

This method does have potential pitfalls. The biggest is to never stop trying to bring additional companies into the development phase. If there is only one company and that company decides to cancel their own project, the start-up may be without a company to pay for the bootstrapping. Second, the development team may focus on the lone customer and develop a product that is very specific to them and not be able to morph it into a general market product.

This method is similar to having the funding available to directly develop the product. Step 1 is to define the product. Step 2 is to identify target customers. Step 3 is to contact those potential customers and present the product. If prospects have the problem and it's severe enough, they will be willing to listen. Step 4 is to have a follow up meeting to discuss funding. Step 5 is contract negotiations. When dealing with joint rights, it's best to leave the details of the terms and conditions to the corporate lawyers. Step 6 is to deliver on your promise and keep in mind these customers may need to be your references in the future.

The second approach of offering contact and consulting services will not directly support the development of your product. If the start-up is developing a social media product, they might be offering software services in the social networking market so it's not completely unrelated. Like the first method, its advantage is financial. Contract fees are typically 2 to 3 times that of in house wages and costs. This will allow the start-up to pay their staff and use the additional revenues to fund development for the general market place revision. The drawback is this method will slow the development of the product, as staff is diverted to contract work.

The third approach of reselling similar products will not ease development of the product, but will provide benefits to the marketing ad sales efforts later. It provides access to the customer base, a great asset in understanding the customers, establishing relationships, and defining the required feature set. Note that customers are willing to say more truths to a reseller because in the minds of the customer, the reseller is disconnected from the provider.

Overall, bootstrapping can slow the development of the product. Start-ups can be distracted by performing on contract obligations and selling. It takes the focus away from the product. However, it forces the start-up to build a company, and groups and skills earlier than a purely investor backed start-up—such as customer service. If the start-up eventually takes funding from investors, they will more likely obtain the funding on more favorable terms. How do start-ups choose a path? In places like Silicon Valley where investor-backed start-ups abound, an entrepreneur's first thought is finding investors; only if investors aren't found do start-ups follow the bootstrapping path. In places where investor-backed start-ups are unusual, the first approach is bootstrapping. An enlightening statistics is that in the last 1,000 companies achieving IPO status, only 60 percent of them were ventured backed, which makes alternatives to investor funding very viable.

Business Model
and Planning

One of the Most Popular Business Models Is the Freemium for You?

Price is what you pay. Value is what you get.
—Warren Buffett

What is a Freemium business model? A Freemium business model offers free basic services and then offers additional or enhanced services as an upgrade for a fee. The premium users pay for all of the users who use the service or product for free. It is a widely used business model in Internet and software business. Whether users are aware of it or not, most Internet users have used a Freemium model product or service. There is a big difference between being a consumer of such a product and being an entrepreneur considering a Freemium model for your start-up. Few know how to implement the Freemium model and get the results needed to sustain a business. When does the Freemium make sense and what can an entrepreneur expect from offering a Freemium model?

The first case study is a software-as-a-service start-up whose product allows users to organize and file away all things digital— a modern day version of the filing cabinet, junk drawer, and moleskin notebook rolled into one. Two years after launching the product, the start-up has 3 million users, of which 60,000 have purchased a premium subscription. That's

2% of the users becoming paying customers and 77% of the paying users choosing the annual subscription fee of $45 over a $5 monthly charge. The company break-even point is at the 1% conversion.

What did their ramp up in traffic look like? After two years, they are signing up 8,000 new customers per day. The drop out and retention rates have remained consistent since the product's launch. In the first month after signing-up for the free version, 50% to 60% of the users abandon the service and never return. In the second month, another 5% to 10% of users leave. Afterwards, the dropout rates dwindle to very small numbers and most customers stay thereafter.

The number of users converting from a free user to a paying subscriber is nil in the first month of usage. After twelve months, the conversion rate between free and paying customers is 2% and after 24 months, the conversion rate is 8%. The start-up attributes the increased conversion rate to the fact that the more information a user enters into the database, the less likely a user will leave and recreate their database on a competitor's tool — this is the traditional lock-in scheme that makes changing for transferring progressively harder. In essence, customers use the service for free for quite awhile before paying. It took 15 months to get the first one million users and 9 months to get the first 10,000 subscribers.

While more than 80% of the start-up's revenue comes from premium subscriptions, they are licensing their technology to other companies, accounting for 10% of the revenue. Advertising contributes another 4%, and the rest is miscellaneous. Initially licensing was a much greater portion of their revenue, but licensing growth has slowed as premium subscriptions are growing. The company revenue is $0.25 per user per month and their operating expenses are $0.09 per user per month. In comparison, Walmart, known for offering rock bottom low prices to the multitudes, collects about $46 per transaction per month.

The start-up has concluded that the following features allow the Freemium business model to work for them:

(1) Good long term retention rate
(2) Customers' perceived value of the service increases as they use the tool more and become more entrenched in its usage.
(3) Low cost and non-variable subscription rates
(4) Expenses require them only to capture single digit percentages of subscribers, who are willing to pay a small amount for the service.

Does this hold true for other companies? A popular social gaming start-up also uses the Freemium model. Their product launched four years ago; they have more than 8 million users with only 5% paying for premium access. This start-up uses micro-payments for revenue and only a small percentage of the paying customers spend $500 a year at the online gaming site. Another start-up targeted at the online dating services is in the early stages of developing traffic, and they 10% of their users become paying customers. Adobe Acrobat for PDF's is an earlier version of the Freemium model. Users can obtain free PDF readers and users must buy the software to create PDF documents.

Not many start-ups can survive on the Freemium model alone; most need a revenue mix to create a sustainable business — subscriptions, advertising, technology licensing, merchandise, and other services. Advertising is usually one of the important components for an Internet-based company, but this too requires volumes. Advertisers become interested in website when traffic reaches 600,000 visitors, though large advertisers want traffic at one million visitors and the largest advertisers look for three million visitors. Companies running blogs or website farms with thousands of sites under their direction only look for daily revenues in the dollars. No matter how one looks at Internet business, these companies require volumes.

Many investors dislike the Freemium business model. They view it as evidence of an undefined marketing strategy, and too often it is just a way for the entrepreneur to postpone figuring out how to sell the product. The Freemium business model works, but only under specific conditions. What can be concluded: it works when the product is a widespread technology whose use is desired by the masses. While we have all heard that the world has become one of niches, these small, specialized markets cannot support a viable business when only pennies of revenue per customer can be generated.

The Detailed Business Plan ... Keep It Simple and Stop Procrastinating

Plans are only good intentions unless they imme-
diately degenerate into hard work.
—Peter Drucker

Most people don't like writing the detailed business plan, yet conventional wisdom recommends doing so. Too often, people procrastinate. They pass it off to someone else in the organization or they hire a freelancer. It is a requirement one would rather not meet, but must do to satisfy investors or creditors. Rather like eating vegetables with each meal, it's what you SHOULD do but you do not WANT to do. It is a dreaded task and once it's completed, you will be measured against its milestones—or it will be shelved.

What causes this reluctance? When you are a start-up, everything needs to be researched, created, calculated, and justified. It can sometimes seem overwhelming; where do you start? You pull out a book or buy a software package, but still there is a nagging question in your mind: couldn't your time be used more productively? Most business plans guides are focused on helping every size and type of enterprise, and for a start-up, most of the information is simply not available or not applicable. Asset value? Day one of the start-up was just yesterday—*what* asset value?

The business planning process should help one understand the business. Yet the very act of writing a business plan can sap one's passion for the new company. Start ups are all different; some are simpler than others. The business plan can be developed in stages to meet the real needs of the business. Just admit that whatever plan you come up with today will not survive the market, customers, or investors. This is your company's best guess. The real question is: Do you have enough of the answers to move forward? Initially, writing the business plan should make your company aware of what you don't know, what you need to learn, and what assumptions you are making about your business. Some answers can be uncovered only in the future. If your company is less than a few months old, how valid are your pricing schemes or market penetration numbers? Not at all.

Everyone knows a start-up will change its plans and it typically requires several iterations. One start-up I was involved in wrote its first business plan after it had been in operation for 18 months, after the 2nd CEO was hired. They presented the plan at a company-wide meeting and the CEO told the employees not to take stock in the volume or revenue projections because they had pulled them out of thin air. They needed numbers to present to potential new investors for the next funding round. Unable to raise another round, the start-up was acquired shortly thereafter. The start-up wasn't acquired for those numbers; the acquirer wanted the technology as a loss leader with attracting customers to its main product line. But knowing you are making up numbers adds to the reluctance — we need numbers, therefore we create them. Savvy investors already know the market numbers, and they have read the market analysts reports. Presenting bogus numbers can do more harm than good; if the start-up is caught fabricating numbers, then investors naturally wonder: What else is false or misrepresented?

There is a better, less daunting way to write a business plan. Keep it simple. The process should guide you to discover the answers to questions to access the technology, the market opportunity and the execution plan needed to realize the vision.

Answering a simple set of questions is a good start. Don't guess at the numbers; it won't help. Don't guess at knowing the customers. Do primary research and contact the customers as much as possible.

Business Vision

- What are the short- and long-term objectives of the business?
- What are the key success factors?
- Why is this a compelling opportunity?

Product

- What will the first release of the project or product look like when it's done?
- What are the minimum things this product will need to do?
- If the first release of the product is a success, what will the next 1 or 2 releases look like?
- What factors will give you a competitive advantage? Unique? Propriety?

Competitive Analysis

- Who are the competitors whose products perform the same purpose?
- What are your competitors' feature strengths and weaknesses, pricing strategies distribution methods, and promotion strategies?
- What is your competitor's market share?
- What is the cost of the total solution or experience to the customer, and where does your product fit into this value chain? What are the individual components of the value chain today? How much of the total solution does your solution address, most start-ups focus on one aspect?
- What are some of the key metrics for your competitors?

Understanding the Customer

- Who are your target customers and why are they the right customers?
- What are your customers' problems and how would your customer prioritize these problems? How do you know your customer problems are real? How do you know if anyone cares about getting this problem solved?
- Will your product features solve these problems?
- How much will the customers pay to solve those problems? In the case of some consumer products, will your product make the customer feel better? Safer? Happier?
- How will customers judge your product, as well as your competitors'?
- Is your product a must-have or nice-to-have product?

- Do you understand how your customer conducts their business or their day-to-day lives?

Marketing Strategy

- How will the customer become aware of our product?
- How will the customer find us? Or how will you find the customer?
- Why would the customer buy your product? Why now? Why not buy the competitor's product? Why not buy nothing and continue doing whatever they do today?
- What partners will we need in this project? Why? Marketing partners? Content creation partners? Business partners?
- What method did you use to determine the price? How important is price as a competitive factor?
- How will you know if the plan is working?

Sales

- What is your best guess for realistic sales expectation and how does it ramp up? What is the low estimate you are confident you can meet no matter what happens? What did you base these numbers on?

Business Model

- How big is the market? How many customers are there?
- How do you make money?

- How will we share revenue between any partners we may need?
- What other items could we sell these customers later? How can you incorporate more of the value chain into your product and capture a greater portion of the total solution?
- What's your profit? Cost should be scrutinized more so than price because cost is under the company's control, whereas price is determined by the market.
- How are you going to build the volumes needed to get to your revenue model?

Execution and Operation

- How can you create a prototype really fast? A start-up's first release is often demo-quality only or just good enough to satisfy the first paying customers. Ask yourself, what is the smallest or least complicated problem the customer will pay us to solve?
- What tools, materials, or people we will need to build this product?
- How long will it take?
- What are the milestones that measure a start-up's progress? Publicly announced and touted milestones should be those that increase the value of the company. Private milestones should be tracked — if you can put a milestone to the activity, why is it being done?
- What do we need to worry about?
- What's do you need to address now? What do we need to worry about down the line?
- What do you need to do next to get yourself moving forward?

- Where do you expect to be a year from now?
- When you exit the company, what do you want the speaker announcing your departure to say about your contribution to the company?

Team

- Who will do the work and what role will each person play in the organization?
- Who do you still need to find?
- Who's going to manage the project and make sure the tasks get done?
- Who's going to advise the company in areas where you lack expertise?

Finances

- What's the least amount of money you need to test the waters for your project?
- How many customers do you need to make your company efficient?
- How many customers do you need to be cash flow positive?
- If the project is successful, what's the funding plan?

Exit

- Can you think of which 10-15 companies would be interested in acquiring your start-up?

See? That's not so terrible. These are a business plan's essential elements. This exercise will help identify the needs of the business because as the saying goes: "A plan without resources is a hallucination."

As time passes and more information is gathered, the business plan will evolve into the traditional textbook version and become honed as the company matures. It's just important that you start somewhere and start answering basic questions about what, why, when, where and how. If the plan is going to be presented to investors then put it into a format investors expect. At the very least, write an executive summary in the standard format because that is one document investors will read.

Example and Outlineof an Executive Summary

Company Name

Company Tagline or Slogan

This should closely follow the company's name. It sets the tone and frames the start-up in the reader's mind. It's underused, but highly effective. One such slogan is "A Technology That Makes Computers Immune to Viruses, Hacking and Spyware". The reader immediately gets a notion of what is to come in the rest of the executive summary.

Company Overview (One or two sentences)

What is the purpose of the company and its vision?
How the company would be classified, what type of product or service does it offer, and what specific market segment does it address?

Examples:

SMB Software is a web-based employee scheduling system which brings workplace management software to the individual small business owner. Our aim to become the compliance software for franchises worldwide, and then address individual restaurants and cafes.

Solar Flex sells the world's first durable, flexible and lightweight silicon solar cells to improve photovoltaic applications.

Problem Addressed or Market Opportunity (One to four paragraphs)

What is the problem being addressed and what is the severity of the problem?

What is the solution and its value proposition?

Start-ups imply technology. This section needs to be explained in terms that everyone can easily understand. One suggestion is to take any documentation already written, hire some freelance writers and let them create these words from this documentation. First, professional writers are simply better than most people at conveying information succinctly. You don't want to get overly involved in describing the problem and its solution, but it can't be vague and general either. Second, it will show what an everyday reader, not intimately familiar with the product, will gleam out of the longer documentation. The freelance writers can easily be hired through websites such as elance.com.

Business Model (One or two sentences)

How does the start-up intend to make money? How will the product be sold?

Examples:

The Twizzle platform offers a license to customers for a monthly fee coupled with revenue sharing on incremental sales from our applications and algorithms.

Sundial sells direct to the customer via websites with our current average selling price of $5.50 per watt.

Hollywood software launched with an annual license of $50,000, and we are introducing a free-to-license-API program.

Cyber Sentry products range from $40,000 to $200,000 per appliance. We sell to distributors, resellers, and managed service providers.

Competing Products (One to three sentences)

What is the general competitive landscape? Mention the name of any direct competitors. Mention any indirect competitors and why they are not in direct competition. Are there any other technologies providing customers with a solution today?

Example:

The main competitors are mechanical aerator providers such as Mecaer, plus a few emerging biological solutions providers including BioFilm Solutions and AquaWorld, all of which focus on larger scale deployment and the retrofit markets.

Market

What is the addressable market size? Is it growing? What is the geographic location of this market?

Example:

The market for pump station control is estimated at $2 billion. We will focus on the USA, UK, and Australian markets, where the number of pump stations in the USA is 250,000, the UK is 35,000 and Australia is 10,000.

Customers and Market Validation

Who are the target customers? If the start-up has current customers, who are they?

Examples:

Currently, there are over 500,000 users engaging our applications through online websites.

WebHealth serves consumers, health providers and health plan organizations. We are already serving a national non-profit and a university. We are in sales talks with over 40 organizations, including 3 of the top 5 health plans.

Intellectual Property

How many patents has the start-up filed and where?

Examples:

One patent filed, but not granted and another six patents in process.

We have a patent pending on the social product recommendations aspect of our technology.

It's best to avoid listing patent numbers in the executive summary.

Key Milestones Achieved To Date
List three key milestones and when they were achieved.

Examples:

Jasper obtained FDA 501 clearance and passed FDS Manufacturer Audit.

Blue Tip won the Best of New Product award at the Global Wireless Tradeshow.

Bright Medical built a team and product in less than one year. We have one system in the field and two systems undergoing installation. Bright Medical has signed 3 strategic partners and has been awarded one government grant.

Development Schedule

What is the current status of the product? Is it under development and when will be the first release? Is there a working prototype?

Example:

We have a working prototype that demonstrates that malicious code is irrelevant and is currently being evaluated by several government agencies. The initial feedback we received was positive.

The first version of the product will be available and ready to be deployed in beta sites in 15 months.

Sales and Profit Projections

Techvation will reach break-even in less than two years. We anticipate achieving $10 million in annual sales in 2 years and expect to surpass $40 million in annual sales after 7 years of operation.

Team (One or two sentences per team member)

List the key team members, what their roles are in the start-up, and what have they accomplished in their experience that's relevant to this venture. Avoid providing a list of titles from previous job positions; it's more about their accomplishments.

Investors and Financing (One or three sentences)

What is the funding to date, how is it structured, and who are the investors?

What funding is the start-up seeking now and what is the intended use of proceeds?

Examples:

We are seeking $3.5 Million dollars in equity-based investment capital from one or more investors in exchange for no more than 40% of the new corporation's ownership interest.

We have raised approximately $3.3 million in convertible notes in the first round. To complete our product design for the mass market, we are raising $10 million in the next round of financing which we expect in two traunches. We are also pursuing government grant money to avoid dilution.

Proceeds will be used to establish a source of distribution in the US, to develop manufacturing in target markets, to develop a presence in Thailand and N. Africa, and expand the product range.

Contact Information

Contact Person, email address, and phone number

Funding Plan

The four most expensive words in the English language are,
'This time it's different.'
— Sir John Templeton

The financial information is part of the planning process that most people dread. It's not especially difficult, but most people suspect that some of it is mere hocus pocus — especially when the start-up is at the concept stage and has created nothing yet. Everything is contingent upon people being hired, suppliers being found, events happening as anticipated, and much more. The financial and funding plans seem like a house of cards. The numbers are guesses. Can you make your listener believe that your financial plans are reasonable and valid? Do you have enough experience and research behind the numbers to make them believable? The key lesson about business planning and evaluation is to never challenge the *numbers* but instead to challenge the *assumptions* on which the numbers are based. Most readers of start-up financial statements glance at the numbers and then go straight to the footnotes to read the assumptions; the readers also know the numbers are hocus pocus. The funding plan is very important, as it shows when and how the company will be funded until it is self-sustaining. Eventually, the funding will need to extend into scaling the company but that plan comes later. This shows the total investment needed to bring the company into the marketplace.

Why are your listeners so intent on the financial statements when everyone knows they are the start-up's best guess? One of the biggest reasons a company fails is lack of capital. Many start-ups get their seed round of funding and breathe a sigh of relief. However, it gets harder to get the next round and even more difficult to get the round after that. These financial statements allow the start-up to develop a funding plan, a roadmap of when the next round needs to be in place to continue operating. Very few companies have a strong enough management team with the credibility to obtain enough funding in the early round to create a long runway; most get only enough to operate for about a year. Second, the lack of working capital can stifle a company's growth—and the competition can expand much faster. A start-up needing to purchase or manufacture expensive equipment before it effectively rents it on a monthly basis to customers can easily suffer a working capital crisis. Third, it often takes just as much capital to solve big problems as it does small problems, and the big problems are simply more lucrative from the investors' point of view. If the start-up is developing an integrated circuit component for medical equipment, the development expenses will be the same for developing a component for the personal computer market. The former will be a low volume product with a high price; it will need to comply with more government regulations, will require the start-up to capture the majority of the market to be a sustainable business, and will be in a slow growing market. The latter may have the opposite characteristics. Which would you invest in?

There are four standard financial statements. The entrepreneur can obtain software, hire a financial professional, or consult a business book to create them. This is how the statements translate in reality to the investors.

- Breakeven Analysis i.e. when does the start-up no longer need investors to pay for the operating expenses? What is the total investment needed for this project?

- Projected Cash flow i.e. when will the start-up need more money and how much will the start-up require at each point, what is the funding roadmap, and how does funding line up with the anticipated milestones?
- Projected P&L is a Pro Forma Income Profit & Loss Statement showing projections for your company for the next three to five years, i.e. can the start-up be sold based upon revenue or profit numbers? For how much? When?
- Balance Sheet is a projection of assets, liabilities, and net worth of the company at the end of next fiscal year i.e. how much can the start-up be liquidated for if it doesn't succeed?

Timing is everything in capital markets. It may take 10 years for an investor to see a return on investment. A start-up's ability to raise funding over the time horizon is uncertain. The volatility of the public markets greatly affects the start-up's ability to obtain capital, go IPO, or negotiate a merger and acquisition. The global financial system is complex and inter-related, and no one can accurately predict it. The only certainty is ups and downs.

Exits and Value Creation

Affairs are easier of entrance than of exit, and it is of common prudence to see our way out before we venture in.

-Aesop

The primary interest of investors is to make money, but they know at the concept stage the exit conversation is too early. The exit strategy is tricky. If the investor harps on it, the strategy may become a metric by which the start-up becomes focused. Shouldn't the entrepreneur be dedicated to building a company and not thinking about the payoff that may be years away? That said, investors want some inkling as to how they will get their profits. Many will want a list of 10 to 15 potential acquirers with reasons why they might consider the start-up; a list of 3 to 4 potential acquirers is too short. Any dialogue about what may happen in 8 to 10 years when the start-up is looking to exit is mostly wishful thinking.

Angels are not under pressure to exit. Angels and private investors are accountable only to themselves and spouses. They prefer companies with an early exit strategy. Unlike venture capitalists, angels will accept dividends. Venture capitalists are fund managers. They invest other people's money and therefore are accountable to investors. If an entrepreneur pitches to a private investor, the private investor makes the decision. If a founding team pitches to a venture capital firm or other professional investment firm, the person you are speaking with in turn must justify the investment to others in their firm and eventually to their shareholders. If your start-up fails, the venture capitalists will be accountable. This makes the venture capital firm far more selective in choosing portfolio companies. The good news about such a monetary outlook is even though an investor may state that they will consider only targeted markets, the reality is different. If they think they can make money with an exit sooner than other start-ups, they will invest regardless of the market segment. Look at all the Y2K funding, which certainly could be considered an opportunistic play with no future potential.

The large venture capital firms look for scalability, growth, and big exits. The smaller venture capitalists, seed to early stage firms, and angels look for several good, small investments. The problem with defining the expected return on investment is changes for current investing climate. What is funded today on the downside of economic conditions would not have been funded ten years ago at the peak of the high tech boom. At the peak, projects requiring $100 million to $300 million were commonly funded. Many seed funding rounds reached between $3 million to $10 million. No investor was interested in the smaller projects. It was a time of big projects, big investments and big returns. Today small is in vogue. Investors are looking for projects with total lifetime investments of $3 million to $5 million and a typical seed funding round is now less than $500,000. Now is a time of smaller projects with smaller, but less risky returns.

Entrepreneurs are often asked, "How will you generate more value for the company?" This is not a question about revenue, but about making the company itself more valuable. Milestones should increase the company's valuation. Milestones are also important to customers; it shows that you can deliver on promises and alleviates the risk of doing business with an unknown. A word to the wise—make a milestone public only if you *know* you can accomplish it or you are close to completing the milestone. Meeting milestones builds credibility; missing them builds doubt. The best time to look for funding is after a crucial milestone is met. If a start-up is asking for its first round after several years of operation, the start-up needs to talk about the milestones achieved during that time. While the investors will ask the start-up about milestones, the entrepreneur should do likewise to the investors—ask what milestones must be met to receive the next round of funding.

Entrepreneurs are usually asked about the company's valuation. This makes no sense to anyone at the concept stage other than to evaluate the response. More than likely, the appropriate response is, "As an entrepreneur, I am focused on building a company. It's the investors' role to set the valuation." Convertible notes are a common means of funding at the earliest stages of a start-up. The very definition of this financing vehicle is that the valuation will be set at a later date. These investors, often angels or private investors, provide funding under the agreement that when the valuation is set, they will receive their exact portion of equity at a discounted price at some future date.

Not all venture capitalists are actively investing. While all invest when times are good, some pull back in bad times. A tactful way of asking a VC is they are actively funding is to ask when they raised their last fund. Funds invest all their money in the first 4 to 5 years, and the remaining years are devoted to managing, scaling the company, and harvesting the portfolio. VCs have 8 or more years before a start-up will exit today and they must maintain cash in funds to support later insider rounds. One rule of thumb for a venture capitalist is the amount of money they expect one company in their portfolio to return is equal to the value of the fund. If a venture capital firm has just closed a $400 million fund, then they look for one start-up to return $400 million to the fund on exit.

What expectations should an entrepreneur be aware of these days? Not all investors are equal and the founders must find those that match your start-up's potential and goals.

- It's not unusual for a start-up to exit with 80% of the company owned by the investors, and 20% for founders and employees.
- Angels want deals with a total investment of no more than $3,000,000. Typically they want 25% to 30% of the company for less than $500,000. An angel's biggest concern is that their share portion of the company will be next to nothing as the later rounds dilute the company's stock.
- Seed stage venture capitalists are more in line with 5x to 10x ROI versus one big home run.
- Some venture capitalists expect the company to sell for $50 million to $75 million for an investment of a few million. Others consider a $50 million buyout too small and want acquisitions of $150 million or more yielding a 3 to 5 times return.
- Mergers and acquisitions with start-ups are historically cyclical. The M&A cycle is five boom years followed by 2 to 3 bust years.
- Start-ups anticipating an initial public offering in the near-term will need a minimum of $100 million or more in revenue, $10 million or more in net income, and 30 quarters of net income.

- A company creating a new market might be unprofitable for 5 or more years, while one in an existing market might generate cash in 12 to 18 months. The expectations reflect this giant chasm between the various types of technology and start-ups. In some companies, the investors look to reach break-even in 3 to 5 years. Others investors are looking for $50 million in revenue in 3 to 5 years with a possible breakout to $500 million or more in revenue.

The definition of exit is the act of going out or away. Not all exits end with success. It simply means it reaches a conclusion. When I worked for a Fortune 500 company, there was a formal spring and fall business planning process. Fall planning was budget allocation; projects presented their business plans and funding was allocated for the next year. Spring planning was budget raiding; projects had to present status against previously stated milestones—inevitably, projects were running short on funds. Therefore, projects were prioritized in the spring, and the less promising projects were shut down and their remaining funds diverted to the projects with a greater potential. It wasn't that the shut down projects couldn't succeed, but the higher priority projects needed the money and there was a greater chance of returns. Venture capital funds have the same problem. The fund may not only provide capital for a start-up today, but also earmark money for that start-up at a later date. Portfolio companies can be over budget and over schedule, and funding needs to come from somewhere. Remember, just as a start-up must show progress to the investors, the investment funds must show progress to their investors. So guess what? Funding is a limited, finite resource.

Odds and Ends

*Indecision brings its own delays, and the days
are lost lamenting over the lost days. Are you in
earnest, seize this very moment.; what you can do,
or dream you can do, begin it. Boldness has genius,
and the power and magic in it.*

— Johann von Goethe

Innovation

Start-ups are all about innovation and technology. Where there is a belief in future profit, there is a funding tsunami and there is progress; the greater the profit, the greater the progress. If the innovation is a success, it will inspire imitations. Competition eventually eats away the profits from innovation, but it's a slow process taking 15 years or more, and by then the next innovations have brought more profits. It is like the ebb and flow of the ocean pounding on the shores.

Innovation comes in waves. Investors fund the latest promising technology. This may be a new emerging technology or an existing technology poised to make a great leap forward. The funding cycle lasts four to five years. The later in the funding wave a start-up begins, the higher the bar is to get funding. Once the wave has been funded, that's it: it's done. Investors then watch and wait, harvesting those with high potential and weeding out those that show little.

Everyone desperately wants to be first with cutting edge technology, everyone desires the latest. But when the next marvelous wonder arrives, it is resisted bitterly — both by investors and customers. Most people simply cannot imagine that the new fangled technology can make people's lives easier or better. It often seems easy and more efficient to keep doing things the way they are done today than to learn to use something new.

Most innovations fail. If the new technology makes it to the market at all, most disappear quickly. Only a very rare few succeed; only 0.036% of companies ever reach $1 billion in annual sales.

Marketing

Marketing wants to make the product stand out in the crowded market. Marketing is taught in business school as a rigorous discipline. Textbooks outline techniques, approaches, and step-by-step procedures. Businesses have organizations devoted to marketing, segmented into areas of expertise with numerous corporate guidelines and requirements. For all marketing's worthy goals for establishing what is different, products blur in the minds of the customers—the products all seem the same. Companies use the same methods for promoting and advertising products. Can you recall any memorable commercials recently? Marketing produces sameness; products seem to coalesce around a similar set of features, thereby rendering feature-by-feature comparison charts useless.

Experience

While venture capitalists and investors have an affinity for the serial entrepreneur with previous start-up experience and a track record of prior start-up successes, the home runs usually come from the first time entrepreneurs.

Funding

There is no secret to funding. It really is a matter of identifying an opportunity, wrapping a business model around it, and constantly searching for those who believe in your idea. The real funding hurdle is understanding what the investment community wants and how the investment community operates — not all investors are the same. You can't just ask the investment community these questions and get straightforward answers. The most common response is they don't know what they specifically want, but they will know the right opportunity when they see it. In any conversation, you will get a pearl of wisdom here and there, but you will not get a concise, concrete picture at one time.

The investor is searching for the right business proposal and "right" is subjective. The entrepreneur is searching for an appropriate investor. Both are looking for the right opportunity. A strong team, a great product, and an exceptional business plan still won't get one funded by a particular investor. One venture capitalist with a sense of humility has the Anti-Portfolio: the successful start-ups they rejected that became household names and stellar companies.

The mistaken belief is that start-ups need funding from investors. Most don't necessarily need it. Plenty of companies have broken through the barrier of $250 million in annual sales without taking venture capital funding.

Product

A start-up need not identify a product that is a disruptive technology in an emerging market. W. Chan's blue ocean strategy concludes the biggest opportunities occur when businesses venture into undefined markets with unknown pricing, whereas the bloody red sea strategy occurs when businesses compete for margins in crowded markets with similar products. Even Dr. Seuss would have great difficulty convincing investors to fund the Super-Zooper-Flooper-Do machine, but it's definitely a game-changing device. Peter Drucker believes the best opportunities are those that are visible but not yet fully *seen*. Business analysts may categorize something as a wondrous product in retrospect, and praise the founders for their brilliance. The truth, however, is the entrepreneur does not define such a product with keen foresight at the beginning. The product emerges and evolves slowly over time.

The Start-Up Plan

What have we all been taught as children? Think about what you are doing before you do it, come up with a plan, focus on the tasks one step at a time, and complete the project. However, this approach just doesn't work well for start-ups and can often stifle the project.

Every start-up needs a plan. By definition, a plan is a series of steps taken to achieve an objective. Most business plans cover a 3 to 5 year period and the goal is broken into intermediate, smaller milestones. Once something is measured and tracked, the focus often becomes performing against the metric. The original plan is not what will get the start-up to the goal. The business plan is a living document, but somewhere along the way it becomes cast in stone — non-living. Everything about a start-up is uncertain, and the plan must grow up: change and improve as more is discovered about the business. Yet the start-up team is judged by the milestones achieved in a timely and efficient manner, which distracts the team from evolving the plan to build a successful product and company.

Respect

Whatever an entrepreneur accomplished in the past may get them funding and respect from investors. Start-ups get no respect from the marketplace. This is often a shock to most first time entrepreneurs, for they are very passionate and proud of their start-up. When I worked for IBM, I used to set up outside partnerships to develop, manufacturer, deliver, and support low volume product options to the customers. The products were sold through the IBM channels. The goal was to not have a contract, commit no volumes, and provide no funding to the partner—nothing promised, nothing guaranteed. Yet whenever I put out invitations for proposals, I got a nearly 100% response rate from potential partners. Everyone wanted to do business with IBM. It's the exact opposite with a start-up and not just with the potential customers. If I am looking for an outside service to do some work, most do not want to do business with a start-up, even if the start-up will pay the same rates as any other customer. People don't return your phone calls. If people wanted to know you in the past, they don't want to know you now.

Selling in Silicon Valley can be challenging. There are some non venture-backed start-ups in the valley that cannot sell their products in the Valley. This may seem odd, but companies in Silicon Valley are so accustomed to venture-backed start-ups that there is an expectation of offering products to initial customers free of charge. Companies outside the valley have had the same experience. Start-up companies that must actually sell their wares for money cannot offer their goods for free; these start-ups must pay their bills by sales.

41531409R00131

Made in the USA
Lexington, KY
16 May 2015